Night of the Living Dolls

Joel A. Sutherland

ALSO BY JOEL A. SUTHERLAND

The Haunted series

The Nightmare Next Door

Field of Screams

Ghosts Never Die

Night of the Living Dolls

To my Bronwen,

who adores playing with her doll collection

and has spent every night since she was

born with Cindy Lou, her favorite.

Apologies in advance if this

book ruins all of that.

Cover design by Vanessa Han
Cover images © Amy Weiss/Trevillion Images; Vinko93/Shutterstock;
Stanislavchuk_Mykhailo/Shutterstock
Internal design by Travis Hasenour/Sourcebooks
Internal images © YaroslavGerzhedovich/Getty Images,
Donald Iain Smith/Getty Images

Published by Sourcebooks Young Readers, an imprint of Sourcebooks Kids
P.O. Box 4410, Naperville, Illinois 60567-4410
(630) 961-3900
sourcebookskids.com

Originally published in 2018 in Canada by Scholastic Canada Ltd.

Library of Congress Cataloging-in-Publication data is on file with the publisher.

This product conforms to all applicable CPSC and CPSIA standards.

Source of Production: Sheridan Books, Chelsea, Michigan, United States
Date of Production: August 2020
Run Number: 5019615

Printed and bound in the United States of America.
SB 10 9 8 7 6 5 4 3 2

CHAPTER 1

"WOULDN'T IT BE FUN IF you were a doll like me?"

"Zelda, your creepy doll is weirding me out," Camryn said.

It was a rainy Sunday afternoon, and we were stuck inside, hanging out in my bedroom. We'd pretty much exhausted all of our conversation topics—school, parents, boys, sports, movies—when Camryn, my best friend, found my doll, Sadie Sees, tucked behind the pillows on my bed. Camryn had pulled the string on Sadie's back that made her talk, and the doll had uttered one of her three phrases.

"Like, why would she want me to be a doll?" Camryn continued. She tossed Sadie to the foot of the bed as if holding the doll physically repulsed her. "Given the choice, wouldn't—what's her name?"

"Sadie," I said casually, trying to make it sound like Sadie didn't really matter much to me.

"Right. Wouldn't Sadie think it would be more fun to be a human...like me?"

"I don't know," I said with a shrug. I really wished Camryn hadn't found Sadie. From then on, I wouldn't be able to keep her on my bed, even hidden under pillows. "She's just an old toy my grandma gave me."

"Why do you even still have her in your room? You're thirteen! I would totally die if someone found something like that in my bedroom."

I closed my eyes and took a deep breath. I was sitting at my computer desk, thankful that Camryn couldn't see my face. She was my best friend—we'd known each other since kindergarten—but lately we'd been growing apart. It was like she was purposefully trying to push my buttons and get under my skin on a nearly daily basis.

Once I had reset my expression with a smile, I turned and faced her. "I keep it for the nights when Lucy has a nightmare and wants to sleep in here. Sadie calms her down."

"If I were you, I'd tell Lucy to keep the freaky doll in her room," Camryn said.

Yeah, well, you're not me, are you? The thought was loud and clear in my head, but I was relieved I hadn't said it aloud. Instead, I stood and crossed the room to pick up Sadie—I didn't want to talk about her anymore—but Camryn quickly scooped her back up before I reached the bed.

"I want to see what else Sadie sees and says," Camryn said.

She looped her finger through the ring on

Sadie's back and pulled the string. It slowly wound its way back into Sadie's body. Her large eyes moved from side to side, and her mouth opened and closed completely out of sync with her words.

"I wish you and I were twins," Sadie said in a high-pitched, warbling voice.

"You are so weird!" Camryn shrieked in the doll's face with a laugh. She looked at me with a wide grin. "Come on, Zelda. You have to admit that she's weird."

I looked at Sadie, unsure how to respond. She looked so helpless in Camryn's hands. Her pink dress was bunched up, and I wanted to fix her short brown hair—it had gotten royally messed up when Camryn had tossed her and picked her back up.

"Sure. She's a little weird," I said even though it pained me to say it. I reached for the doll but Camryn pulled her back.

"Oh, no, no, no, no, no," Camryn said with a shake of her head. "I'm not done with her yet." She pulled the string again.

"I can see through anything," Sadie said.

But something was wrong. Her voice slowed down and deepened as she spoke. Her mouth stopped moving and her eyes locked in place, staring straight ahead—straight at Camryn.

"Nope!" Camryn shouted. "Not cool. Not cool at all." This time, instead of simply throwing Sadie to the foot of the bed, she pitched the doll off the bed. I heard Sadie thump on the floor.

"Can we talk about how your doll just became possessed by an evil demon or something and tried to kill me?" Camryn said.

"Settle down. Sadie didn't try to kill you. She probably just needs new batteries." Even as I said it I knew that couldn't be right; Sadie didn't run on batteries.

I stood to retrieve the doll, but Camryn raised her hand, stopping me.

"How about we just leave her down there?" she said.

"Sure. If it will make you feel better, we can

leave my possessed doll on the floor beside the bed, you big baby," I teased.

Camryn smiled and gave me a playful shove. "I'm the big baby? I'm not the one who sleeps with a dolly. Where's your pacifier, Zelda? Where's your blankie?"

"Like I said before, I keep the doll in here for—" I didn't finish the sentence.

Sadie Sees interrupted me.

She skittered across my bedroom floor—from the side of the bed to my computer desk—like a giant insect.

Downstairs the telephone rang, loud and piercing in the silence. Camryn screamed.

Sadie lay on her side silently staring at us from across the room. But a new shuffling sound came from directly under my bed.

And whatever was under there sounded *big*.

CHAPTER 2

CAMRYN PULLED THE BEDSHEETS OVER her head. Without waiting for an invitation, I joined her under the sheets. It wasn't a particularly brave reaction, but I wasn't feeling particularly brave.

Camryn's whole body shook, and her eyes were wide. "What was that?" she mouthed silently.

I shrugged and wondered what was going to happen next. Would Sadie attack us—as unbelievable as that sounded—or would the thing under the bed be the first to strike?

With nothing but a thin sheet protecting me from the horrors in my room, I felt incredibly helpless.

"Zelda." A small voice in the room called my name.

"Hear that?" Camryn placed a hand on my shoulder and gently shoved me to the edge of the bed. "Whatever's out there wants you."

I couldn't tell if she was joking or serious. I swatted her hand off me and, luckily, she didn't put up a fight.

"Zelda," the voice said again. This time I recognized it.

I pulled the sheet off my head and saw my sister standing right in front of me.

"Lucy?" I said. "What are you doing in my room?"

"Hiding under your bed," Lucy said plainly, as if there was nothing odd about that at all.

Camryn pulled the sheet off her head. Her hair was frizzy with static electricity. "Wait.

What? Lucy? Have you been in here, like, the entire time?"

"No, not the entire time," Lucy said defensively. "Just since...um...a little before you two came in."

"Could you hear us?" Lucy nodded.

Camryn sighed, buried her face in her hands dramatically, and said, "Great, just great. Now a nine-year-old kid knows all of my deepest, darkest secrets."

"Don't worry. I didn't hear all of your secrets," Lucy said. "Just that you have a crush on Derek McCreary, and your mom is taking you to buy your first bra this weekend."

Camryn threw back her head as if she'd been slapped, and opened and closed her mouth rapidly. She looked a little like a fish trying to breathe out of water, and I took the smallest shred of satisfaction in seeing the shade of red that spread across her cheeks. For the first time in ages, she was at a loss for words.

"Did you slide Sadie Sees across the floor?" I asked Lucy. The doll was in the exact same spot as before—I kept stealing glances at her just to make sure she hadn't moved again.

Lucy nodded. "Why?" I asked.

"I don't like her. She should be called Sadie Scares."

Camryn laughed once loudly, more of a bark. "Busted! I thought you said you kept Sadie in your room for Lucy when she has bad dreams."

"I don't have bad dreams," Lucy said quietly, her face scrunched up in confusion.

I ignored that and steered the conversation back to the fact that Lucy had been in my room since before Camryn and I came in. "Why were you hiding under my bed? You should've come out ages ago. We've been in here nearly an hour."

She laced her fingers together and held her hands low, then cast her eyes down to the floor. "I don't know. I was bored, I guess."

"All right, well, you know what?" Camryn said, slipping off the bed. "As much as I love being spied on by your little sister, I think I'm going to go."

"You sure?" I said, looking out the window. It was dark, gray and very, very wet. "It's still coming down pretty hard out there. I can ask my parents if you can stay over for dinner."

"Thanks, but I'm good." Camryn crossed the room quickly, eager to leave. She paused with her hand on the doorknob. "Just do us both a favor and get rid of that creepy doll." She eyed Sadie briefly, then ripped her gaze away from the doll and glanced back at me. "Especially since you're not fooling anyone when you say you're hanging on to it for her." She cast her eyes at Lucy, then turned and left the room.

I walked to the door to follow her, then decided she'd be fine seeing herself out.

The sound of her footsteps on the stairs was followed by the opening creak of the front door, the pitter-patter of rain hitting the front porch, and the slam of the door.

"Sorry if I made her leave," Lucy said.

"Don't worry about it," I replied, and I meant it. A year ago there was no way Camryn would've cared whether or not I had a doll on my bed. In fact, until recently she'd had a stuffed unicorn that she brought to every sleepover. But in the past few months it was like she had purposefully set out to grow up in a hurry.

I shoved my concerns out of my head and smiled at Lucy. "C'mon, let's go downstairs and see what's for dinner."

Lucy nodded eagerly. "I'm starving!"

We walked downstairs and found the house to be oddly silent. An unsettling and unexpected feeling of apprehension suddenly came over me, a feeling I couldn't explain.

I led Lucy down the hall, popping my head into the family room, living room, and dining room along the way. All empty.

The kitchen was empty, too, and no one had started dinner. Nothing on the stove, nothing in the slow cooker, and no veggies chopped up on the cutting board or meat thawing on the counter.

"Where are Mom and Dad?" Lucy asked.

"I don't know. Maybe they went out?"

"Check the fridge," Lucy suggested. "They always leave a note when they have to run out."

But when I checked I found the refrigerator door bare.

I checked my phone in case I had missed a message. I hadn't.

The feeling of apprehension exploded inside me, adding anxiety, fear, and panic to the mix.

Calm down, I told myself, *and think back*.

I remembered something. While Camryn and I were in my room, Lucy slid Sadie Sees across the floor, and then...

"The phone rang just once," I told Lucy. "Back when Camryn was still here. And when she went home, I didn't hear Mom and Dad say goodbye to her. Maybe they got a call and had to leave."

I noticed that the red light on the wall phone in the kitchen was lit, indicating someone in the house was on the line.

A loud and pain-stricken moan suddenly came from the screened-in porch.

It was Mom.

It sounded like she was being murdered.

CHAPTER 3

I RUSHED OUT BACK WITH Lucy close behind. Mom was bent forward on one of the patio chairs with her face buried in her hands. Her body was heaving, and she was crying loudly.

Dad was sitting beside Mom. He was holding one of the cordless phones to his ear.

"I know, we're in shock, too," he said. He looked up and saw my sister and me standing near the patio door, then gave a sad little nod that I couldn't quite read—but I knew it wasn't good.

"I'll tell her, and I'm sure she'll call you when she's able to talk," Dad said to the phone. "Okay, take care of yourself. And again, I'm so sorry."

That's when I knew what had happened, even without Dad saying anything else.

"Thank you. Bye," Dad said, then he hung up. "Kids," he said to us. It looked like he wanted to say something else but didn't know where to start. He wasn't sobbing like Mom, but he looked emotionally drained.

"What's wrong?" Lucy asked.

Mom looked up. Her eyes were red, and her cheeks were covered in tears.

Lucy and I went to her. She hugged us both and then confirmed what I had feared.

"Grandma Edith passed away this afternoon," she said.

"She's dead?" Lucy asked in shock.

Mom couldn't speak; she could only nod. Fresh tears sprang from her eyes. She dried her face with the back of her sleeve.

Lucy's face bunched up, and she began to cry. "Come here, sweetheart," Dad said, guiding Lucy to him. She wrapped her arms around his neck and sat in his lap, then buried her face in his chest and continued to cry. He rubbed her back and kissed the top of her head.

"We heard Mom from the kitchen," Lucy said, her voice muffled by Dad's chest. She raised her head and said, "It sounded like you were dying!"

"I'm sorry, love," Mom said with a smile full of woe. "It took a bit of time for the shock to wear off, but when it did... Well, I'm sorry if I scared you."

"Mom is just really sad," Dad said. "So am I."

It felt like an hour had passed, but in reality it had only been a minute, maybe less. I was numb. So numb that I didn't even feel sad. I just...I couldn't believe it.

"You okay, Zelda?" Dad asked.

I nodded, but I wasn't okay. I was in shock. Grandma Edith was my last living grandparent, and I thought she'd live forever. She was old, but she was also still very strong and independent.

"How did she die?" I asked. My voice cracked.

"The hospital believes she had a stroke," Dad said. "She died quickly. They don't think she suffered much."

I loved visiting Grandma's house in Summerside. It was only about an hour away, so we visited lots. She lived in a small yellow house that was filled with knickknacks and old wooden furniture, and felt so cozy in the winter and calming in the summer. Every time I'd gone to her house she would greet me on the front porch, rain or shine, sun or snow.

Other than my parents, she was the only person who remembered that I liked my sandwiches cut into squares instead of triangles. She taught me how to bait a fishing hook and grow tomatoes and told the best bedtime stories, filled with ogres and knights and dragons and princesses.

I stopped myself—or tried to stop myself—from thinking of Grandma in the past tense. I hated how it reminded me that she was no longer part of my present, and would never be part of my future, either.

But I couldn't stop thinking that way once I'd started. Tears sprang from my eyes, and I found it a little hard to breathe. Dad still held Lucy, so Mom pulled me into a tight hug.

"It's okay, Zelda," Mom said. "Your grandmother had a good life, and she wouldn't want us to be sad."

"What happens now?" Lucy asked.

"We're going to go to Summerside," Dad said. "There's a lot to be done."

"But we have school tomorrow," Lucy said.

"We'll call the school first thing and tell them what's happened," Mom said. "They'll understand."

"Where will we stay?" Lucy asked.

"I just got off the phone with your Aunt

Joyce," Dad said. "She and Uncle Greg offered to let us stay with them, but their apartment isn't big enough for all of us. We'll stay in your grandmother's house."

"So we'll be gone all week?" Lucy asked quietly.

"Probably," Dad said with a nod. "The funeral will likely be Friday, and Grandma wanted it to be held in her house."

Lucy frowned. She looked scared. She whispered so low I had to strain to hear her. "I don't want to stay there, not without Grandma. I'm scared."

CHAPTER 4

"WHAT WAS THAT, LUCY?" DAD asked, tilting his head to the side in confusion. He squinted and looked to Mom, then back to my sister. "Did you say you're scared?"

Lucy's bottom lip quivered, and her cheeks flushed. "No! I said I'm sad. I don't want to go to Grandma's if she's not there." She covered her face with her hands and started to cry. Dad wrapped his arms around her.

"It's okay," Mom said. "It'll be tough for all of us."

An awkward silence fell on the room. It lasted a little too long. I tried to think of something to say to make Mom feel better.

"I'm so, so sorry, Mom." It was the best I could come up with.

Mom looked at me and nodded with a sad smile.

She looked like she wanted to cry but held on.

"All right," Mom said. Her voice cracked a little. "Let's order a pizza, pack our bags, and try to get to bed early tonight. Tomorrow's going to be a long day."

I tossed some clothes, toiletries, and books in my suitcase and set it by my bedroom door. That done, I walked down the hall and poked my head into Lucy's room. She was lying on her bed, surrounded by pencil crayons, working on a Harry Potter coloring book.

"Hey, Lucy," I said. "Is it all right if I come in?"

"Sure," Lucy said without looking up. She was pressing the pencil crayon to the paper with more force than necessary, and was coloring quickly and messily.

"You okay?" I asked.

Lucy paused for a second or two, then continued. "Yes."

"It's just...you seem a little agitated. If you keep coloring so hard you're either going to break your pencil crayon in half or rip through the paper and decapitate that poor hippogriff."

She continued coloring without answering.

I sat on the edge of her bed. "If you're scared, you're not the only one. I'm scared, too."

That got her to stop. She dropped the pencil crayon and crossed her arms.

"You get scared?" Lucy asked doubtfully.

"Of course," I said.

"What are you scared of?"

I said the first thing that popped into my head. "Bears."

Lucy laughed a little, which was good. "Bears?" she asked.

"Definitely. Aren't you afraid of bears?" Lucy shook her head.

"Well, you should be. They're very dangerous. If one walked into the room right now I'm pretty sure you'd learn to be scared of bears really quick."

She laughed some more, a little louder this time, but soon looked serious and thoughtful again.

"Zelda?"

"Yeah?"

"Are you afraid of anything other than bears?"

Something in her eyes—a mix of hope, fear, and sorrow—made me answer truthfully and without pause. "Yes," I said. "I'm also afraid of going to Grandma's house tomorrow. I'm afraid being in her house without her there will be too upsetting. I'm afraid it will make her death too real." My chest ached. It felt like someone had reached a hand inside my body and squeezed my heart.

"But what if she's not really, *really* gone?" Lucy asked.

A chill spread down my back. Years ago I'd watched an episode of *Screamers*, and I'd sworn I'd never make that mistake again. In the episode there was this little kid who repeated, "The dead don't die. The dead don't die. The dead don't die," in an eerie voice, which gave me nightmares for weeks. And here was my younger sister saying something eerie in real life, which was far creepier than anything a TV show could produce.

"I know you're upset, Lucy, but Grandma is really, *really* gone."

"I know," she said quietly.

I nodded in sympathy and squeezed her shoulder. "I don't think we should be scared of

Grandma's house. It's just a house. It might be nice to see Grandma's things and be around her stuff. What do you think?"

Lucy didn't look completely sold, but she also didn't look quite as upset as before. She nodded. I'd take that as a win.

"Good." I stood up and opened a dresser drawer, then pulled out a few T-shirts. "All right, let's get you packed." I looked out my sister's window. The sky was black and full of stars. It was getting late. I stifled a yawn. "Like Mom said, we've got a big day tomorrow. We should get some sleep."

Preferably nightmare-free, I thought as the *Screamers* kid's voice echoed in my mind: *The dead don't die. The dead don't die. The dead don't die...*

I really hated that show.

CHAPTER 5

I SHOT UP IN BED with a gasp. I'd had a weird dream, but whatever it had been about was gone as soon as I opened my eyes.

Lucy was standing beside my bed. "Sorry!" she said, sounding shocked.

I took a few deep breaths and let my heartbeat return to normal. I leaned back and placed my elbows on my pillow—it was soaked in sweat. "It's fine. I'm fine. I had a bad dream, that's all. What's up?"

"It's almost time to go. Mom asked me to wake you up."

I hopped out of bed, pulled on the same shorts I'd worn the day before, and looked at myself in the mirror. My hair was a mess. I pulled it back and tied it into a ponytail with a hair elastic as I made my way to the bathroom. Lucy followed. I turned on the tap and splashed some water on my face.

"All right," I said. "I'm all set."

"Aren't you going to shower?" Lucy asked.

"I just did."

Lucy laughed. "Well, you better come downstairs soon or else Mom and Dad will get mad." She turned and left.

I returned to my room and grabbed my bag, then paused in the doorway and looked back at my bed. Sadie Sees's hair was poking out from under a fold in the comforter. I picked her up and stared at her eternal smile for a moment. I unzipped my bag and nearly placed her in it, but then paused and put her back on the bed.

Wait a minute, I thought. *Camryn won't be there, but Grandma will.*

I packed Sadie Sees and flew out the door. It wasn't until I'd reached the bottom of the stairs that I realized I'd forgotten that Grandma was gone.

All the more reason to keep Sadie close.

We pulled into Grandma's driveway. Dad killed the ignition, and a heavy silence descended on us. We'd stopped to pick up lunch a few blocks away, and the greasy smell of hamburgers filled the car.

It had smelled good a minute ago, but not so much anymore.

The midday sun was at its peak in a clear, blue sky that was far more cheerful than our moods. I had to shield my eyes as I looked at Grandma's pale yellow house. Bay windows jutted out on either side of the front door, which was constantly shadowed by an overhang and tall bushes. A sloping cellar door on the side of the house led to the unfinished basement. I pictured the backyard, where I'd spent many hours playing outside, which was walled off from the empty lot behind the house by a row of tall cedars. Somehow, despite all of its quirks, Grandma's house had always felt like one of the most comfortable and inviting places in the world.

But the house didn't feel comfortable or inviting at that moment.

We grabbed our bags in silence and walked slowly to the front door. Mom stopped and put her bag down before setting foot on the porch.

"You coming in?" Dad asked.

Mom shook her head. "Not right now. It's so nice out." She tried on a smile, but it faltered and fell from her face almost immediately. "I'll join you in a bit."

Dad nodded, picked up Mom's bag, and waved Lucy and me into the house. We dropped the bags in the front hall and closed the front door, leaving Mom alone outside. I could still see her through the small window on the door, but the glass was tinted and bumpy, so she looked red and blurry.

"Who's hungry?" Dad asked.

"I am," Lucy said. She carried the food down the hall and into the kitchen.

"Coming?" Dad asked me.

"In a bit," I said. "I'll...um...take the bags upstairs."

Usually he'd say something like "Food's not going to get any warmer," or "You're going to waste away if you don't eat." But this time he simply said, "Okay," and patted my shoulder. Then he joined Lucy in the kitchen.

I stood alone in the front hall.

Make yourself at home, my dear. I heard Grandma's voice in my head.

On my right was a bathroom, a small dining room, and the kitchen in the back. On my left were the living and the family rooms. In front of me was the staircase to the second level and the attic. I looked at the bags but decided to leave them for a moment and wandered to the left.

I walked into the living room first. The floor, baseboards, door, and window frames were all made of dark wood. The furniture was large and brown. Everything was so cozy even though the colors in her house were very dark. I happened to catch a glimpse of Mom through the window. She was sitting on the front porch swing staring at the garden.

The floorboards creaked as I walked into the family room, which was always my favorite place in the house. Grandma had a TV in there, sure, but what I loved most was the large brick fireplace. It burned real wood, not like the gas fireplace we had at home, and the smell of the smoke was the best. Grandma never seemed to like the fireplace. But she knew I loved it, so when I visited she'd humor me by lighting a fire on cool evenings.

Grandma's reclining chair was just as I always remembered it: large, brown, and covered with a blanket. On the small table beside the chair were her reading glasses and an open book placed face-down. Was it the last thing she read? Was that the last thing she did, period? I hadn't asked where Grandma was or what she was doing when she'd had her stroke.

I wiped at my eyes and left the family room.

The bags weren't going to carry themselves upstairs (a variation on another one of Dad's favorite sayings), so I grabbed my bag and Mom's and took them upstairs.

The door to Grandma's room was closed, which was a relief—I wasn't ready to go in there yet—so I tossed Mom's bag and my own in the other bedroom. She could move hers later. Although we hadn't discussed where we'd all sleep for the week, I figured my parents would be in Grandma's room, and Lucy and I would share Mom and Aunt Joyce's old room.

I studied the narrow staircase leading to the attic door. Something made me hesitate. I shook my head and walked up step by step. Each one groaned, and one or two were so loud that I thought they might crack in half. I opened the door, walked to the middle of the dark, windowless room, and pulled the string to turn on the overhead light bulb. *Click-click!* Pulling it reminded me of Sadie's string, and I heard her voice in my head. *I wish you and I were twins.*

One of the first things I saw in the light was the flashlight on the floor beside the door, kept there to light the way to the string. "Right," I said to myself. "Next time."

The attic had floor-to-ceiling wood, and its curved ceiling reminded me of the hull of an old boat, like a pirate or Viking ship. Shelves lined the room and were packed with stuff—some in bins, some not. Old clothes, purses, and shoes. Paintings, records, and books. Tons of scrapbooking supplies. Piles of holiday decorations.

An entire bookshelf of my grandmother's journals, dated and arranged in chronological order.

In the corner, nearly buried by a pile of old clothes, was an old-fashioned trunk. I'd stumbled on it one day when I was my sister's age. Inside the trunk were six super-old dolls. None of the dolls matched, which for some reason made me feel uneasy. They seemed jarringly out of place in the trunk, like they didn't belong in there. The day I discovered them, Grandma caught me just as I was about to pick one up. She yelled at me to stop and slammed the trunk shut, nearly pinching my fingers. Once she'd caught her breath, her face returned to normal. Then she explained that the dolls were antiques, quite valuable, and too fragile to touch. She asked me to never open the trunk again. I'd promised, but I guess she still felt bad for yelling at me, because the next day she gave me Sadie Sees.

I'd had really weird, vivid dreams that night. In them, the dolls had walked and talked. They had wanted to do something bad to me, something I couldn't quite remember by morning. And I'd also dreamt that I'd looked through Grandma's bedroom window in the middle of the night and saw a large stone building, like her house had been picked up and moved to a big city or something. Like I said: weird.

Even though discovering it had gotten me Sadie, the trunk was the only thing in Grandma's house that I didn't like. The only thing that scared me a little.

I hadn't seen the trunk in years. Maybe Grandma had hidden it. Or maybe I'd avoided it on purpose.

But there it was, what I could see of it. It was made from dark wood, and the rounded lid was covered with stones that looked like bright-red cranberries. And although I couldn't see the odd assortment of old dolls inside the trunk, I knew they were there. Not seeing them was worse than if they'd been splayed out on the floor.

I wiped some dust off the red stones and then heard something, something that sounded sort of like laughter. Children's laughter.

I turned around, thinking Lucy must've followed me up, but the attic was empty. Just me and the dolls.

I turned back to face the trunk. The lid rattled.

CHAPTER 6

I JUMPED BACK. MY GUT felt like it had twisted into knots.

The trunk's lid had rattled. I was sure of that. Well, mostly sure.

But how could that be? Maybe I had imagined it. Or maybe there was something trapped inside. An animal?

If there was an animal trapped inside it, I needed to let it out.

I took a deep breath and placed my hands on

the lid. I heard Grandma in my head yelling at me for opening it just as she had done years ago. I flipped the lid open and quickly blocked my face with my hands, just in case there was a raccoon or a family of opossums or something hiding inside, ready to pounce.

Nothing happened.

"Huh," I said in the darkness.

I peered into the trunk. It was nearly empty. All that it held were the same six antique dolls that had been stored in it before.

That settled it: the rattling must've been in my imagination. I laughed a little and took a closer look at the dolls. I hadn't had time to examine them in detail the first time I'd found them.

One looked like a big baby. She wore a bonnet and had a pacifier in her mouth. Another looked like an old woman with curly gray hair and metal wire-framed glasses. One was neither female nor male. It had a blank face and a flap in its torso that opened to reveal plastic organs inside, like it was used to teach human anatomy or something. One was a girl with eyes much too large for her face and set too low. Her ceramic skin was cracked around the left eye and the corner of her mouth. Another was made completely out of wood and had posable limbs, with joints at the ankles, knees, waist, wrists, elbows, shoulders, and neck. The final doll was old, like the others, but in much better shape. It was a pleasant-looking girl with curly red hair, a few freckles on each cheek, and blue eyes. She wore an emerald-green dress that looked nicer and fancier than anything I owned.

I reached into the trunk and pulled out the doll in the green dress. She was heavier than I expected. I turned her over and saw that someone had written a name on her calf: Hattie.

"Is that your name?" I asked the doll, turning her back around to look at her face. "Hattie?"

The doll winked and I dropped her. She landed with a dull thud on top of the other dolls in the trunk. I quickly slammed the lid shut. I shivered as a slight feeling of revulsion rolled over me.

Almost as quickly as it had happened I realized that, like seeing the lid rattle, the wink must've been in my imagination. I opened the trunk again. I picked up Hattie once more and noticed that her eyes opened and closed when I tilted her up and down, which made it look like she was awake when upright and sleeping when lying down.

"For a second there I thought you were alive," I told Hattie with a laugh. "And here I am now, by myself in the attic, talking to a doll." I tossed her back in and put my hand on the lid but hesitated before closing it.

There was a small loop of dark-red ribbon sticking out from between the bottom of the trunk and one of the side walls. I slipped my finger into the loop and tugged it. The foot of the trunk lifted up, causing the six dolls to tumble to the opposite side and revealing a secret compartment beneath.

Hidden away were two items: a school yearbook and a journal. Why wasn't this journal kept with the others on the bookshelf? I removed both books and turned my attention to the yearbook first.

The cover read SUMMERSIDE SCHOOL 1952 in gold foil. Above this lettering was a stamp of what I assumed was the school emblem.

There was a picture of the school on the first page. It was a tall stone building, three or four stories, with large windows and a bell tower that jutted up to the sky above the front door. It was creepy, like a classic haunted house, but larger and more intimidating. I couldn't imagine going to school in a building like that.

On the next page was a letter from someone named A. Ashton, who was listed as the school's headmistress. I glanced over the letter and learned that Summerside School was a private institution for "girls from the finest families from our country and beyond," and that the school had a "sterling reputation for educating and shaping tomorrow's women."

I flipped through the pages and saw black-and-white pictures of teachers and children from kindergarten to eighth grade. I closed my eyes and did some quick calculations. Assuming the yearbook was Grandma's, she would've been eight years old in 1952 and probably in second grade. I turned to the page of second graders and scanned through the students' faces until, sure enough, I found a picture of a familiar-looking girl with the name *Edith Fitzgerald* printed beneath it.

I had a hard time picturing Grandma going to a school like Summerside. It seemed so prim and proper, and Grandma...wasn't. She was more of a practical, hands-on, no-nonsense kind of person, and her family hadn't been wealthy, either. I recalled her once telling me her father had been a janitor, and that after he'd died her mother had worked two jobs to pay the bills and avoid losing their house.

I was about to close the book when I happened to catch the name of one of my grandmother's classmates: Hattie Craick.

Had Grandma named her doll after a girl in her class? And what about the other dolls? Did they also have names?

I pulled out the baby doll and turned it end over end. There weren't any markings on her, but under her clothing I found a different name written on her back: Mary. I examined the other four dolls and discovered each one had a different name written somewhere on it: Dorothy, Virginia, Lois, and Ruby.

I turned my attention back to the yearbook and found four matching names: Dorothy Kearns, Virginia Coxwell, Lois Hershey, and Ruby Rosswell. Why would Grandma have dolls with other girls' names on them?

And then it dawned on me: the handwriting was different on every doll. Grandma hadn't named the dolls after her friends from school. The dolls had *belonged* to those six friends from school.

CHAPTER 7

THERE WAS DEFINITELY SOMETHING ODD about the whole thing.

Holding the dolls made me feel really sad. Like they were full of negative energy that left me feeling cold, both physically and mentally. I put them back in the trunk, closed the lid, and hid the yearbook behind it. I picked up the journal, still feeling an overwhelming sense of sorrow.

I needed to get out of the attic. I needed fresh air. I took the journal and quickly walked down both sets of stairs. Avoiding Lucy and Dad in the kitchen, I passed through the family room and went outside through the sliding door. I closed it quietly and took a deep breath with my eyes closed. The sun felt warm on my skin, and the breeze blew through my hair.

After three more deep breaths, I opened my eyes. The first thing I saw was the tall, dark hedge at the far end of the backyard. The breeze grew colder, coating my skin in goose bumps. A shadow passed from left to right through the hedge. Probably a neighborhood kid playing on the other side. Lucy and I had always enjoyed playing there, too.

On the other side of the hedge was an empty field—empty except for the ruins of a large stone fireplace and chimney, the last remnant of some long-forgotten building. I loved that fireplace. It was so old and mysterious. I'd asked Grandma about it once, and she said it had been there as long as she could remember. I wondered if it could've once been part of a wealthy family's mansion, or maybe it heated a wing of a small private castle. In my imagination that fireplace had been the center of many adventures.

Sudden movement interrupted my fantastical thoughts. A shadow paced back and forth behind the hedge, like a ravenous animal stalking prey. It was too big to be a kid or an animal. A chill tickled my skin and made me shiver. The wind died down, and I heard the sliding door open behind me. It was Mom.

"Hey, kiddo," she said.

"Hey, Mom." I slid the journal under my leg, hoping she hadn't caught sight of it.

"You haven't eaten yet," she said.

"Nope."

She eyed me sympathetically and with a hint of concern. "Are you okay?"

"I'm okay. It's a little weird being here, I guess."

"I know what you mean. Why don't you come

in and eat with me? Your father and sister are already done, and I could use the company. Maybe some food will make us feel a little better."

"Sure thing," I said. "I'll be in in a minute. Cool?"

A little smile tugged at Mom's lips. "Cool."

She closed the door and stepped out of sight.

That had been a close call. I didn't want anyone else to catch me with the journal, so I hid it beneath the deck and glanced at the hedge. Whatever had been on the other side was gone.

Later that night, I was startled out of a deep sleep.

I didn't know what had woken me up. It wasn't that I had a bad dream. I wasn't hungry or thirsty. I didn't have to use the bathroom.

Something was in the room with Lucy and me. My sister was sleeping soundly on the twin bed next to mine. Whatever had entered the room hadn't disturbed her.

I sat up and gripped the bedsheet tightly in my hands. The room looked empty, but I had that feeling in the pit of my stomach that told me I was in danger, and that other feeling on my back that made me think I was being watched. A thick blanket of clouds had rolled across the sky outside my window, blocking the moonlight. I couldn't see much detail outside the small circle of red light from the digital clock on my bedside table. It read 3:01 a.m.

A blur of movement passed over the far wall. Shadows from the headlights of a passing car on the street, I tried to convince myself.

The floorboards creaked—just once, but loud enough for me to be sure it hadn't been my imagination.

"Hello?" I said. "Is anyone there?" Silence.

My breaths—short, fluttery little gasps for air—were awfully loud in the stillness of the night. I waited and watched for another moving shadow, waited and listened for another floorboard creak. Nothing happened.

I dug under the bedsheet for Sadie Sees, but my fingers didn't find her. I reached a little deeper and still came up empty. I could've sworn I'd had her when I first got into bed. Maybe I'd knocked her out of bed while I was asleep.

An ice-cold breeze passed by the side of my bed, and the drapes ruffled as if moved by the wind, but the window was sealed shut.

"I know someone's in here," I said suddenly. A tear sprang from the corner of my eye, and I brushed it away in a panic. What would Camryn think if she could see me now? I didn't care. All I wanted was for the nightmare to be over.

Suddenly an office chair in the corner of the room began to spin rapidly all on its own. With each revolution, it made a hair-raising, high-pitched squeak that sounded almost like a human scream: *eek-eek-eek!*

I shut my eyes tight and buried my face in my palms, wishing I had an extra pair of hands to cover my ears. The squeal of the chair was grating.

Eek-eek-eek!

I still hadn't opened my eyes, but I could tell by the sound it was making that the chair was slowing down.

Eek. Eek. Eek.

It no longer sounded so frantic.

Eek. Eek.

And then it uttered one final, drawn-out *eeeeek...*

All was silent.

I peeked through my fingers for a moment.

Nothing moved, nothing stirred.

The clouds outside parted, and a splash of moonlight softened the darkness.

The chair was facing the bed. Sitting on it, staring me down, was Sadie Sees. Her eyes looked...lifelike, like she was actually seeing me.

And then she blinked, smiled and—as if she had read my mind—said, "I can see through *anything*."

CHAPTER 8

"WHAT DID YOU SAY?" I demanded frantically of Sadie. I felt like I was losing my mind.

The doll couldn't have spoken on her own. She couldn't have spun the chair. But there was no one else there except for Lucy, who was still asleep.

I can see through anything. It was one of Sadie's recorded phrases.

Can you see me now? I thought, not daring to ask the question out loud. *Can you see through me?*

She sat as motionless on the chair as...well, as a doll. As a doll *should* be, anyway. But her eyes still had a lifelike look about them, which freaked me out more than anything.

I slipped out of bed and crossed the room, keeping my eyes on Sadie as I slowly approached her. I reached out to grab her but stopped my hand in midair. The doll watched me the entire time. I poked her in the chest to see what would happen.

Nothing happened. Of course. What had I expected—that she would giggle like she was ticklish?

I must've imagined it. Or maybe I was still asleep when I saw the chair spin and heard Sadie talk.

"You need more sleep, Zelda," I told myself as I closed my eyes and rubbed my face.

Eek! Eek! Eek!

I paused with my hands still covering my eyes.

That sound...

Eek! Eek! Eek!

It was the chair spinning again, but I couldn't bring myself to look.

"Whee!" a small voice said. And although it wasn't one of her recorded phrases, I knew at once that it was Sadie's voice.

I finally managed to drop my hands and open my eyes.

Sadie was playfully spinning in circles on the chair and hooting with joy. She looked so happy, so carefree. But she also looked...different. I can't explain how, just different. She was the same doll I'd always known and loved, and yet she was also a complete stranger to me.

The chair stopped suddenly, and Sadie laughed. She brushed her hair out of her face, smiled, and took a deep breath. Her cheeks were flushed. "That was fun," she said. "Made me feel young again. You should join me for a few spins, Zelda."

You know that expression, cat got your tongue? I felt like a big cat—a tiger or a lion—had ripped my tongue clean out of my mouth. Not only couldn't I talk, but I felt like I couldn't breathe, either. I backed away in horror until my legs bumped into the bed, and I stopped, staring at Sadie in utter bewilderment.

"I've got an idea!" she said. "Let's stay here forever, just the two of us. What do you say?"

"No," I mumbled. It was all I could manage. My voice didn't even sound like my own—it was like I'd left my body and was watching from above, like a movie or something. A horror movie, obviously.

"But we can be twins. You can be a doll, just like me." Sadie slipped off the edge of the chair and landed soundlessly on the floor.

"No," I said again, shaking my head. Nothing made sense. Nothing was real. "I'm a girl, not a doll."

"For now," Sadie said, crossing the room toward me. There was something horribly unsettling in her tone and in her eyes—a hint of malice, a glint of madness. "One day, all of this will be over. One day, just like Grandma, you'll die. And then we can be twins. We can be dolls. And nothing will ever tear us apart."

Overcome with terror and panic, I closed my eyes and buried my face in my palms. But something wasn't right. It was the feeling of my palms on my face. Instead of warm and soft, my hands were cold and hard. They felt like plastic. I pulled my hands away and looked down at them. Instead of my normal human hands, they were doll's hands. "No," I said. I looked in the mirror on the wall beside me, dreading what I'd see but powerless to look away.

The skin on my face was smooth and free of blemishes. My hair looked like wool. And my eyes were glass.

I was a doll.

"See?" Sadie said. She was suddenly right beside me. "We're twins. We're dolls. Forever and ever and ever."

Her eyes turned red and her teeth grew long, and she hissed as she lunged with clawed fingers for my neck.

I screamed and bolted upright in bed, then blinked and shook my head.

The room looked slightly different. Sadie was gone. My hands were normal once again.

"What happened?" Lucy asked. My scream must've woken her up.

My heart pounded in my chest. I pushed my hair out of my face and looked around, trying to steady my breathing and my nerves. Sadie wasn't on the chair. In fact, I didn't see her anywhere. I'd been asleep. The whole thing with Sadie spinning the chair and me turning into a doll and her attacking me was a dream. No, not a dream. Definitely a nightmare.

I was about to check for Sadie under the sheets when Mom and Dad burst through the door.

"What's wrong?" Mom asked as she turned on the light.

"Is everyone okay?" Dad asked.

"Sorry," I said. "I had a bad dream and screamed."

Mom gave me a sympathetic nod. "What was the dream about, sweetheart?"

I shook my head. "I don't remember." Truthfully, I didn't think I'd ever be able to forget, but I didn't want to talk about it so lying was easier.

Mom accepted my answer and felt my forehead, as if to make sure I wasn't coming down with something, then turned the light back out.

"All right, girls, try to get back to sleep," Dad said.

My parents left, closing the door behind them.

I listened to their footsteps in the hall, and the click of their door closing, then sighed.

Everything was quiet again, but only for a moment.

In the darkness Lucy said, "You didn't wake me."

"What?" I said.

"You didn't wake me. I woke up a little before you did, thanks to your doll."

"What do you mean?" I asked, confused.

Lucy looked left and right, then her gaze settled on me. "She spoke."

I CLOSED MY EYES AND rubbed my temples, trying to make sense of what Lucy had just told me. Sadie *had* spoken. It *hadn't* all been a dream.

"That's what happened in my dream," I told her. "Sadie spoke to me—all on her own—and then she turned me into a doll, and then she attacked me so that we could be together forever."

Lucy frowned and looked at me as if I'd just sprouted a second head. "She said one of the things she always says: 'I can see through anything.' She didn't do any of that other stuff."

"Oh, yeah, I know," I said, realizing that I'd mistakenly believed Lucy had seen Sadie speak on her own. I smiled and laughed, feeling a little embarrassed but also a little relieved. "I guess I must've moved her cord in my sleep. Weird."

"Yeah," Lucy said, still looking at me oddly. "But not as weird as your dream."

"I found a doll collection up in the attic this afternoon," I said. "Seeing them must have caused my nightmare."

Lucy shrugged her shoulders. "Where's your doll now?" she asked.

"Here in bed where I left her," I said.

I patted the bed on my right and left but didn't feel her. I lifted the sheet and peered beneath, but she wasn't there.

"At least, she *was* here when I fell asleep," I said.

"Huh," Lucy said.

"What?"

"She's here." Lucy pulled Sadie out from under her own sheet.

"How...?" I asked. "Did you take her after I fell asleep?"

Lucy shook her head. "I don't know how she ended up in my bed, but I guess I must've made her talk, not you."

"Yeah, I guess." I held out my hand. "Here. Pass her back."

She leaned over and started to hand Sadie over to me, but then she looked at the doll's face and paused. "Actually, do you mind if I hang on to her? Just for the night?"

"Really?" I said, surprised by the request. Lucy never seemed to care much about the doll, and after the dream I'd told her about, I figured she'd care even less.

She nodded. "For some reason, having her close makes me feel better right now. And...I don't know...makes me feel closer to Grandma. Does that sound silly?"

I smiled, thinking back to the first night after Grandma gave me the doll, and how much better I felt holding her close as I drifted to sleep.

"That doesn't sound silly at all," I told her. "Of course you can keep her tonight."

Lucy thanked me and lay back down. "Zelda?"

"Yeah?"

"Maybe tomorrow night, too?"

I laughed. "Sure."

It took a while, but we both eventually fell back asleep.

I was sluggish and headachy when I woke the next morning, and Lucy looked like she felt the same. We moved around Grandma's house like a couple of zombies, passing each other in the hallway as we shambled from the bedroom to the bathroom to the kitchen, finally settling at the table.

"You both look great," Dad said sarcastically

as he placed bowls of Xtra-Bran Flakes in front of my sister and me.

"Ugh," I said, picking up a spoonful of the brown cereal, which was quickly turning into sludge, and letting it slide free and fall back to the bowl. "Can't I eat some Crystal Crunch or Honey Bears?"

"That's all there is in the cupboard," Dad said. "Any more bad dreams last night?"

"Not that I remember," I said.

Lucy choked down a mouthful of her cereal with a pained expression. "Tastes like twigs."

"How do you know? You've never eaten twigs," Dad said, then frowned. "Have you?"

Lucy didn't answer.

Mom came in and went straight for the coffeepot. She poured herself a mug and leaned against the counter as she took a long sip, then sighed.

"We're going to be out most of the day," Dad said. "We've got to meet up with Aunt Joyce and

Uncle Greg and take care of some other stuff, too. Will you girls be okay on your own for a bit?"

"Of course," I said with a shrug.

Lucy looked too disgusted by Grandma's cereal to answer.

I pretended to eat the Xtra-Bran Flakes while Mom and Dad puttered around the kitchen, then rinsed it down the drain in the sink as soon as they'd left. Despite the fact that she seemed to hate it and had proclaimed it tasted like twigs, Lucy managed to finish her entire bowl. She patted her belly and went back upstairs.

Time passed slowly. I tried to read but couldn't get past a single page. I tried to watch TV but couldn't focus. I tried to eat but couldn't work up much of an appetite. By two o'clock I didn't feel like sitting inside Grandma's house any longer. I went out to the backyard and sat on the edge of the deck, then reached under the wood boards and pulled out the journal.

"What's that?" Lucy asked.

I flinched and squeezed the journal to my chest. "Lucy. I didn't hear you come out here."

She ignored what I said and asked again what I was holding.

"Grandma's journal," I said. "I found it in the attic yesterday and hid it out here."

"Under the deck?" Lucy asked. "What if it rained?"

"I didn't think of that," I admitted, looking thankfully up at the blue sky. "I found it in a hidden compartment in a trunk along with her school yearbook." Now that I'd told my sister that much, I decided to tell her everything. "The trunk had six old dolls in it. There was a different name written on each, and I found pictures of girls with the same names in Grandma's second-grade class. I don't think they were hers."

"Why did she have them if they weren't hers?" Lucy asked.

"I don't know," I said. I looked away. My gaze landed on the back hedge.

The hedge swayed in the wind, and its movements sounded eerily like quiet footsteps and whispers.

"I wish she was here," Lucy said.

"Me too," I said heavily.

We sat in silence for a while, each wrapped up in our own thoughts.

Something moved, a shadow on the other side of the hedge like the one I'd seen the day before. But this time, I could've sworn whatever had been there was peering through at us.

"What was that?" Lucy asked.

"You saw it, too?"

Lucy nodded.

"Someone is spying on us," I said.

CHAPTER 10

"WHO'S THERE?" I CALLED OUT, surprising Lucy. She flinched a little when I spoke.

Whoever was hiding on the other side of the hedge didn't answer.

I stood up and walked quickly across the backyard. I caught glimpses of the shadow winding through the branches and thick foliage as if it was keeping a close eye on us. But by the time I reached the hedge, the shadow was gone.

Lucy joined me. "Did you see who it was?"

I shook my head and pushed my hands through two cedars. The needles scratched and pricked my skin as I dug my hands in deep. I parted my hands and peered through the opening.

On the other side of the hedge was...nothing and no one. Just the empty field I'd played in when I was younger.

"Maybe it was an animal," I told Lucy. I looked up at the clear sky. "Or maybe a cloud passing over the sun."

"Let's make sure," Lucy said.

I didn't really want to leave Grandma's backyard, but I also didn't want Lucy to think I was scared, so I nodded and slipped through the hedge. Lucy followed.

The air on the other side was noticeably chillier. I shivered and felt goose bumps raise the skin on my arms. The hint of an odd smell tickled the inside of my nostrils. It smelled like a mix of grilled meat, copper pennies, and—

"Smoke," Lucy said.

"Excuse me?"

She looked startled by my presence as if she'd forgotten I was still there. "It smells like smoke here."

I nodded. I couldn't remember the field ever smelling like that before. "Someone must be barbecuing," I offered. I looked toward the small houses down the road on Ashton Lane.

"Yeah, maybe," Lucy said, her voice full of doubt.

She followed me into the middle of the field and we turned around, scanning the surroundings. As usual, there wasn't much to see other than grass and weeds and rocks and the old stone fireplace in one corner of the lot.

"No spies," I said.

Lucy agreed. "No animals, either."

And no clouds, I thought. What had we seen? The field was too large and open for the source of the shadow to have run out of sight so fast. The only hiding place I could think of was the fireplace. I pointed at it and said, “Let’s look in there.”

We walked slowly around the fireplace. Moss had spread over the surface of the stones like a green rash, but nothing was hiding behind or inside it.

I placed my hand on the stone to lean into the mouth of the fireplace and look up into the chimney. As soon as my skin made contact, an image flickered through my mind. I saw a large and foreboding building, so vivid that it took my breath away. I flinched and pulled my hand free, and the vision disappeared. It had only been in my mind for a fraction of a second, such a short time that I immediately doubted it had been real.

“What happened?” Lucy asked.

“Nothing,” I said with a forced smile that I hoped looked reassuring. Nothing like that had ever happened before—I must’ve touched the fireplace dozens of times. I clearly needed more sleep. My head started to throb as if a headache was coming on.

I wondered for the first time what had happened to the building that had been reduced to its fireplace. I surveyed the rest of the field, tracing an imaginary line starting at one side of the fireplace, around the field, and back to the other side. There was a pattern in the grass that might've been where the building's walls used to stand. It was hard to pinpoint, but the grass on the "inside" of the building was darker and stood still, while the grass on the "outside" was a brighter shade of green and moved like a gentle rolling wave.

Without thinking I leaned against the fireplace again and once more saw an image flash in my mind, but this time it wasn't a building. Instead my head was filled with roaring flames. I immediately stepped back; the fiery image disappeared, and my head began to pound. I moaned and doubled over.

"Zelda?" Lucy asked, concerned. "You've got to tell me what's going on!"

"I will," I said quietly. "Once this headache passes. But for now, don't touch the fireplace."

The wind picked up once more, this time sounding like a voice that was both far away and uncomfortably close.

Die, it seemed to say, the word drawn out to its breaking point.

Die...

"Do you hear that?" I asked. Lucy nodded.

Die...

"It sounds like..." I said.

"Mom," Lucy finished.

I listened closer. Not "die" but "da."

"Zelda?" Mom called. It sounded like she was on the other side of a wide lake, her voice traveling cleanly over the smooth surface of the water. "Lucy?"

"We're here, Mom!" I shouted back. Lucy and I hustled across the field and passed through the hedge. I hid the journal beneath my shirt.

"Zelda! Lucy!" Mom's voice was much louder the moment we were back in Grandma's yard. "Your father and I were worried sick. When we got back and found the house empty, we thought..." She stopped talking and wrapped us both up in a tight embrace.

I laughed, partly from nervousness and partly from my mom's overreaction. "We were only gone a minute or two."

Mom pulled back and stared at me quizzically. Now it was her turn to laugh nervously as she shook her head. "We came back more than half an hour ago, and we've been looking for you the entire time."

I didn't believe her until she pointed at her watch. It read 2:47 p.m. I'd stepped outside at two o'clock. Mom was right. Lucy and I had been gone for at least half an hour, if not a little longer. But that was impossible.

I smiled and said, “Time flies when you’re having fun.”

Mom smiled back, but she looked a little concerned, too.

She couldn’t have been as concerned as me. Half an hour had passed in a matter of minutes. A small portion of my day was missing.

CHAPTER 11

"YOU'VE BEEN GLUED TO YOUR phone for hours," Mom said after coming into the family room to get one of Grandma's photo albums.

"Just texting Camryn," I said. Which wasn't a complete lie. Camryn had texted me once a little earlier to tell me she was hanging out with Allan and Sam while they played a video game called *Kill Screen* that I'd never heard of. But it wasn't the full truth, either. I hadn't texted her back—what would I say? K thnx?

Instead Lucy and I had been scouring the internet for any clues or information about who used to live behind Grandma's house, and what had happened to the place. The image of the building that had flashed in my mind the first time I'd touched the fireplace was familiar, but I couldn't quite place it.

"It's nice you and Camryn are still such good friends," Mom said.

I didn't really know how to answer that, but luckily I didn't need to. Mom left without waiting for a response.

"Find anything yet?" Lucy asked for the hundredth time.

I sighed. "No, nothing yet."

Lucy was sprawled out on the opposite couch. She got up and sat beside me. "Wait. Why are we searching for clues online?"

"What do you suggest we do instead?"

Lucy shrugged innocently and said, "What about Grandma's journal?"

"Of course!" I said. "Follow me."

"Where to?"

"The attic," I said. "I want to show you the trunk and the yearbook."

I grabbed the journal and led Lucy up to the third floor, then pointed out the trunk in the corner.

"So that's where the dolls are, eh?" she said.

"I hope so," I replied. "Yes," I added. I reached behind the trunk and pulled out the yearbook, which I handed to Lucy.

Lucy flipped through it while I opened the journal and started to skim the entries.

"Find anything important yet?" Lucy asked.

"Not yet," I said. Everything I'd read had been typical little-kid stuff, like what Grandma wanted for her birthday, and how much she loved her parents. But then I turned another page and an old, yellowed newspaper clipping fell out.

"Bingo," Lucy said.

I picked it up off the floor and read the headline aloud: "Street Renamed in Honor of

Headmistress Ashton, One of the Many Who Perished in School Fire." The article was from 1954 and had two pictures, the first of a large stone building with the caption *Summerside School in 1940*. And then it all clicked.

The image of the building I saw when I touched the fireplace was familiar because I'd seen a picture of it in Grandma's school yearbook.

"The fireplace on the other side of the hedge is all that's left of Grandma's school," I said.

"I wonder why she never told us that," Lucy said.

I wondered the same thing and tried to think of an explanation. Then something in the second photo caught my eye. It was a picture of the charred and smoking ruins of the school, with a caption that said the photo was taken the morning after the fire in 1952. But what caught my eye was the hedge—Grandma's hedge, but the back side of it. It was much smaller and more well-groomed. I pointed it out to Lucy because what caught my eye about it wasn't actually the hedge itself, but something else.

In front of it was the distinct outline of a dark, ghostly shadow.

I couldn't sleep that night. Not well, anyway. I tossed and turned, then slept for a bit, then tossed and turned some more, then slept a little more. This went on for hours. The consistent sound of Lucy's deep breathing from the floor beside me got under my skin. Why couldn't I sleep as peacefully as her? Sometime after 2:00 a.m. I gave up trying and turned on my phone.

Camryn had texted again.

hello??? earth to zelda

u forget ur phone or something?

I sighed, then sent her a quick response.

I'm ok. just busy

I considered adding "And, you know, kind of

preoccupied with the death of my grandmother," but decided against it.

I nearly tossed my phone aside in frustration, but instead placed it on the bedside table, on top of Grandma's journal. I looked at the journal in the pale light of the moon. I hadn't read any further, but it felt like the right time. I didn't think I'd fall asleep, so I figured why not?

The yearbook was from 1952, so I flipped through the journal pages until I found an entry dated with the same year about a third of the way through.

I read it.

Dear Diary,

Im sad. Today was bad. I took the cookies Mommy and me baked and gave them to the girls but they did not like them. They said they wood not eat them if they were dieing of hunger or if they were the last food on erth. Hattie took the bag and thru it on the ground and stomped on them and said no one could eat them becuz they were poisen. I asked her what she ment and she said they were poisen becuz they were made in my house and my daddy is the school care taker and we are poor, so the cookies wood be full of dirt and worms and other things humans cant eat.

I dont know why they are so mean. I wish the girls liked me. I just want to be frends.

I sat and stared at the page for a while, confused. I'd assumed Grandma and the girls were friends since they'd lent her their dolls, but the journal entry made it clear they were anything but friends. My confusion quickly gave way to sadness as I pictured Hattie stomping on the cookies Grandma had baked for her. Why would anyone be so mean?

I reread the part about why Hattie said the cookies were poisoned.

> *I asked her what she ment and she said they were poisen becuz they were made in my house and my daddy is the school care taker and we are poor, so the cookies wood be full of dirt and worms and other things humans cant eat.*

Grandma's father was the school's caretaker? I didn't know that. Add it to the list.

"I can see through anything," a voice in the darkness said.

I slipped the journal beneath the waistband of my pajama pants and pulled my T-shirt over it, hiding it instinctively. Then I rolled over and checked on Lucy. She was still fast asleep, and in the crook of her arm was Sadie Sees. She'd held me to my promise to lend her the doll for the night.

"You awake, Lucy?" I whispered.

She didn't answer. She must've jostled Sadie's string in her sleep, like she'd done before.

I rolled onto my back and stared up at the ceiling. *Sleep*, I pleaded with myself, *sleep, sleep...*

"I can see through anything," Sadie said again.

I rolled over and looked at the doll. She stared back at me. Not only was it strange that Lucy triggered Sadie to speak in her sleep again, but Sadie never repeated the same expression twice in a row. It must've been some sort of glitch. I rolled over once again. I wasn't going to fall asleep staring at my sister and my doll. "I can see..."

It couldn't be, not three times in a row. I turned to look as quickly as possible, and as soon as I locked eyes with Sadie Sees she finished her sentence.

"...*you*, Zelda!"

CHAPTER 12

IT COULDN'T BE. IT DIDN'T make any sense. Sadie Sees had looked me in the eye and said my name.

Her eyes were so disturbing. They looked like real eyes—like in that dream I'd had, but this was definitely not a dream.

"I can see you, Zelda," Sadie had said. And something about the look in those human eyes peering out of her doll face made me believe her.

Suddenly I had an uncontrollable urge to laugh, even though there was nothing funny about it.

The doll stared at me silently from Lucy's bed. There was an odd look on her face—like she was thinking.

Lucy yawned and rubbed her eyes. "Zelda?" she said groggily. "What is it?"

My doll, I thought. *She said my name. She said she sees me.*

I couldn't bring myself to say that out loud. A wave of nausea rolled over me.

Lucy sat up quickly, as if she sensed that something was very, very wrong.

Sadie tumbled off the bed and landed face-down on the floor between me and Lucy.

"What is it, Zelda?" Lucy asked, her voice frantic. "You're scaring me." She sprang off her bed as if by catapult, stepping on Sadie before leaping into my bed.

We held each other. I kept my eyes on the doll.

"She looked at me," I said shakily. "She said my name."

"Sadie Sees?"

I nodded.

Sadie's arms spun in their shoulder sockets, and she placed her palms on the floor beneath her chest.

I flinched, and Lucy buried her face into my neck, squeezing me tight. She couldn't watch what was happening, but I couldn't look away.

Sadie pushed her small body up and got to her feet. She looked at me again with her unnaturally real eyes and her pleasant smile that appeared horribly out of place. For a moment we just stared at each other in silence before she spoke.

"Don't be scared," she said. Her voice still sounded like Sadie's recorded phrases, but her mouth moved in perfect sync with her words, and her eyes no longer moved from side to side as she spoke.

"What do you want?" I asked, trying my best to keep my voice steady.

The doll took a step toward me. "I want to be with you, Zelda. I want to be with Lucy, too."

"Who are you?" I asked.

She took another step closer and then paused. She looked left and right and raised a hand to her mouth. Her fingers curled and uncurled, and then she said, "I'm so sorry. This must be terribly frightening for you. I should have told you right away."

"Should've told me what?"

Her plastic smile widened. "I'm your grandmother, Zelda."

For a moment I couldn't speak, I couldn't breathe, and I could hardly even think straight.

"What?" I managed to say.

Lucy pulled her face away from my neck and peered at the doll.

Sadie nodded. "It's me. Grandma," she said. "I know I don't look like myself..."

That was an understatement. "But it's true."

"Grandma?" Lucy asked in disbelief.

Sadie nodded again.

Lucy quivered, as if part of her wanted to give Grandma a hug and part of her still hadn't gotten over the fear and shock.

"What are you doing in Sadie Sees?" I shook my head, not completely able to believe that this conversation was taking place.

"I..." Sadie spread her arms out to her sides and shrugged. "I thought this would be less shocking for you both than if I'd appeared in the night looking...well, like a ghost. I didn't want to scare you, but now I'm not sure this was any better."

"I've missed you, Grandma," Lucy said.

"I've missed you, too," Sadie replied.

Lucy appeared to accept that our grandmother had possessed Sadie Sees, but the thought was so unreal that I had trouble coming to grips with it. I wanted some sort of proof that she was who she said she was.

And then I had an idea.

"If you're really Grandma," I said, "tell me what you hid in the trunk in the attic."

There was a gleam in Sadie's eyes. "Dolls," she said. "Six dolls."

That was a start, but it wasn't good enough. "Anything else?" I asked.

"Did you find the secret compartment in the very bottom?" she asked.

I held my tongue and waited for her to elaborate, not wanting to give away any hints.

Sadie nodded and said, "Clever girl. That's where I hid my yearbook and journal."

I felt a mental wall crumble, and I was overcome with emotion. Tears ran down my cheeks and I wiped them away quickly. "I miss you so much, too, Grandma."

"Sweet, sweet girls," Sadie—*Grandma*—said. "But don't be sad. Now that you know I'm not truly gone, we can still be together... And I need your help."

"With what?" I asked.

“Pick me up and I’ll show you,” she said, raising her arms in the air.

I picked her up and tried not to think about how weird it was to be carrying my grandma. “Where do you want to go?”

“To the attic.”

CHAPTER 13

AS WE PASSED GRANDMA'S ROOM, she held a finger up to her lips to keep us from waking Mom and Dad then pointed up to the attic. Lucy and I crept up the stairs as quietly as possible.

The room was one big pool of shadows. The thought of wading into the darkness of the attic, with the creepy collection of old dolls in the trunk and my grandma's ghost in my own doll, gave me the creeps. I sped to the center and pulled the string. The overhead light made me feel a little more at ease.

I grabbed Lucy's hand—her palm was sweaty, and her fingers were shaking—and gave it a gentle squeeze. As weird as the night was turning out to be, at least we were together, and I wanted to spend more time with Grandma, even if she was a doll.

"Okay," I said, "we're here. Now can you tell us how we can help you?"

I put Grandma down. She paced around the attic, peering around boxes and looking under piles of her own things. "Where is it?"

"Where's what?" I asked.

"The trunk," Grandma said without looking at me or slowing her search. "The one with the dolls, of course."

I frowned. "It's right over there," I said, pointing at a corner of the attic. "Right where it's always been."

Grandma looked at it but stayed where she was in the center of the room. "Open it," she said.

"Why?" I said. That was the last thing I would've

expected her to say. She'd gone to such lengths to stop me from opening it when she was alive.

"I'll tell you why," Grandma said reassuringly. "But first, open the trunk and then everything will make sense."

Lucy started toward the trunk, but I put my hand on her shoulder and stopped her.

"What are you doing?" Lucy asked, confused.

"Yes, what are you doing?" Grandma said, a hint of annoyance creeping into her voice.

More than anything I wanted to believe that Grandma hadn't moved on, that she was in Sadie Sees and speaking to us at that moment. But everything felt wrong. Everything felt off. Grandma wasn't speaking the way she usually spoke. She'd always been direct and to the point, but she'd never been impatient or rude.

"Why didn't you know where the trunk was?" I asked.

"What?" Sadie Sees snapped. I was through thinking of her as Grandma.

"This was your house, right?"

"Of course it was, you silly girl."

If I had any lingering doubts, that made up my mind. "Then how'd you forget where the trunk was, you...whatever-you-are?"

"Stop it, both of you," Lucy said. She sounded close to tears.

"Lucy," Sadie said, "don't listen to your sister. She's confused, which is understandable. This is confusing for all of us. But please, open the trunk." I tightened my grip on my sister's shoulder.

"She's not going to do that."

"Ow!" Lucy said.

"You're hurting her," Sadie said. "Let her go."

I shook my head. Why didn't Sadie open the trunk herself? Why did she need us to do it for her?

"She's not our grandma," I told Lucy.

Lucy shook her head in confusion, but when she looked at me again she appeared to believe me.

Sadie uttered a frustrated groan. "Fine," she said. "We'll do this the hard way."

Her head swiveled to the side, and she looked intently at the overhead light bulb. It started to glow impossibly bright and then, after a moment, the coil inside the bulb popped, and the attic plunged into darkness.

CHAPTER 14

"WHERE ARE YOU, SADIE?" I said. I could hardly see a thing.

Sadie didn't answer.

Lucy squeezed my hand. "Don't leave me," she said.

"I won't," I assured her. "Sadie, where are you?" I asked again, a little more forcefully.

Still no answer.

"Who are you? Why did you pretend to be our grandmother?" I demanded anxiously.

"Why, my dear girl, I'm the headmistress."

"Miss Ashton," I said. "What do you want with my grandma's trunk?"

"Not the trunk," she said, her voice suddenly coming from our right. "What's inside. The souls of the six girls who once owned those dolls have been trapped inside them since they died in the fire. But if they're released from the trunk and returned to the spot where they died, they'll be able to escape the dolls and, well...I wouldn't want to be you if that happens."

"Why not?" I asked.

"Because they aren't too fond of your grandmother," Sadie said.

Lucy gasped and her hand was yanked out of mine. There was a thud a short distance away.

"Truth be told, neither am I," Sadie said.

"Lucy?" I called. "Where are you?"

"I'm here," Lucy said, her voice traveling from the corner where the trunk was stored. "She knocked me down."

"And now do you feel that pressed against your neck?" Sadie asked my sister.

"Yes," Lucy answered.

"That's a pair of scissors, and a rather sharp pair, too, I might add. If you do anything foolish, Zelda, *snip-snip*."

She must have taken the scissors out of Grandma's scrapbooking supplies. I pictured Miss Ashton cutting Lucy and closed my eyes tight in an attempt to rid myself of the image.

"And if you don't open the trunk soon, Lucy, I might lose my temper and do something I'd regret. Well, something *you'd* definitely regret. Understand?" Miss Ashton was quick to add, "If I were you, I wouldn't nod."

"I understand," Lucy choked out.

"Why are you doing this?" I asked frantically, not daring to move. I had my doubts that she'd actually do anything so extreme, but I couldn't afford to take the chance. "And what do you have against our grandmother?"

"Two different questions that are linked by the same sad story," she said. "Ever since the day I died I've been unable to move on. I've been trapped here, in the small area around the school. And to make matters worse, I haven't even been granted the dignity of retaining my human form."

"The shadow near the hedge," I said, thinking of the dark form that Lucy and I had seen. "That was you."

"It was indeed," Miss Ashton said.

That's how she knew what was hidden in the trunk. She must've overheard Lucy and me talking about it.

"All these years—these long, *long* years—I haven't been able to take shape, possess anything, or even speak. All I could do was watch and think. But when you opened the trunk yesterday, that changed, if only a little. I felt a touch of my old strength flow back into my veins. It was as if some of the girls' remaining shred of life was freed into the atmosphere and found its way to me, giving me the ability to take possession of your silly doll."

"But why?" I said, trying to think of a way to release Lucy. This had gone on far too long. "What do you hope to gain by possessing Sadie Sees?"

Miss Ashton laughed with a condescending tone. "I'm going to free the souls from the six dolls in your grandmother's trunk, and by releasing them, I'll gain the favor of the Wisp."

"What is the Wisp?"

"An immortal being, older than time, and a harvester of lost souls. She's the mother of the Netherrealm—the afterlife world—and she's the only entity with the power to grant me what I desire. I will reach out to her through a séance so she can witness the girls' transformation from dolls back to spirits. I have no doubt the Wisp will then turn me back into the woman I once was, or at least shepherd me on to whatever plane comes next."

Very little of what Miss Ashton had just said made sense to me, but I didn't feel like that mattered half as much as the other question I'd asked, so I asked it again.

"What do I have against your grandmother?" Miss Ashton repeated with a spiteful laugh. "Open the trunk, Lucy, and I'll answer your sister's question."

There was a silent pause that seemed to go on forever.

"I. Said. Open it," Miss Ashton ordered.

"Do it, Lucy," I said.

The trunk's old hinges creaked as the lid swung open, and I dreaded what might come next.

I heard the quiet whispers of six excited young girls.

"Thank you, Lucy," Miss Ashton said. "And as I'm a woman of my word, I'll enlighten you about your grandmother. But first... Girls! This is your headmistress. Come out here and join me once more."

I heard a series of small rustling sounds and knew the dolls were standing up in the trunk. This was followed by a brief, whispered conversation I couldn't fully make out. I caught the word "two," and then Miss Ashton told the dolls to "wait until there's one."

Miss Ashton continued speaking to me and Lucy. "Where was I? Oh, yes. Your family is responsible for me being in this predicament. Your beloved grandmother, Edith..." She spat the name out as if it was a mouthful of venom. "She killed me."

I shook my head. "That's insane."

"Is it?"

"Of course it is. You died when the school burned down, and Grandma was only eight years old at the time."

"Eight is plenty old enough," Miss Ashton said, "to start a fire."

CHAPTER 15

I TRIED TO IMAGINE GRANDMA setting the school on fire. It was laughable, ridiculous, and not just at eight years old, but at any age. She was the kindest person I'd ever known. There was no way.

I heard what sounded like six sets of small feet landing on the attic floor, then a soft whimpering from my sister. I felt frozen, unable to do a thing.

"I don't believe you," I said.

Miss Ashton laughed. "You don't? That's fine.

Honestly, I didn't think that you would. But don't take my word for it. Take your grandmother's."

"Is she here?" I asked hopefully.

"No, she was fortunate enough to pass on," Miss Ashton said with a jealous sigh. "The only way you'll see her anytime soon is if some unfortunate circumstance befalls you. Tragic." Miss Ashton shook her head and tsked in an overdramatic way. "I was referring to her journal. I saw you with it. Why don't you see if she shared her deepest, darkest secret in there?"

I removed the journal from my waistband and looked at the cover. It was far too dark to read.

I heard footsteps—small, hollow, plastic sounds—run across the attic from right to left, and then something scraped across the floor and came to a stop when it hit my foot.

"A flashlight," Miss Ashton said. "To help you read."

Although I didn't like Miss Ashton's friendly tone—it was too forced—I bent down and picked up the flashlight and turned it on. But instead of reading the journal, I aimed the light at the corner where the footsteps had led, just as Lucy—now free—rejoined me.

Miss Ashton was at the attic door. The six dolls surrounded her, three on each side. All seven glared at me and Lucy. The sight of them—moving, sneering, and staring fixedly at us—was disturbing.

Miss Ashton pointed the scissors at us.

"If either of you follows us," she said, "I'll cut you up into so many pieces that you'll end up looking like this." She hit the anatomy doll, the one labeled Virginia, on the back with the handle of the scissors. The faceless doll's torso popped open and all of her organs—lungs, stomach, kidneys and heart—scattered on the floor.

Virginia got down on her hands and knees and collected each of the organs, then placed them back inside her chest and sealed the flap up again. She didn't even seem to mind. The other dolls chuckled. What sort of headmistress had

Miss Ashton been? I suspected she had been a pretty awful one.

Or had she turned awful after she died?

"Come, girls," Miss Ashton said. "We have work to do."

The big-eyed doll, Lois, left the attic first, making muffled thumps on the stairs as though she were sliding down the steps on her bum. The baby doll, Mary, was next. Then Dorothy, the old woman, Ruby, the wooden doll, and finally Virginia, the anatomy doll, all followed.

Hattie—the perfect, sweet-looking doll—hesitated, then took a step toward us. "Why don't we just do it now?"

"Hattie?" Miss Ashton said, notes of confusion and concern in her voice.

Hattie took another step as if she hadn't heard her headmistress. "Why bother with the needle and thread?"

"Hattie!" Miss Ashton shouted sternly. "That is enough. Don't you dare say another word."

Hattie finally clued in and blinked as if she was remembering where she was, then turned and followed the other dolls out the door.

Miss Ashton frowned and drew her lips tight, managing to make Sadie Sees's face, always so bright and cheerful, appear annoyed and angry. Who had gotten deepest under her skin? My sister and I, or Hattie?

"As I've already warned you, girls," she said, "don't get any ideas about following us. And don't bother telling anyone about what you saw tonight, either. After all, who would believe you?"

She turned to leave, but paused and added, "Pleasant dreams." Then she stepped into the darkness of the stairwell and was gone.

It took Lucy and me a few minutes to remember how to do something as basic as walk—it's not every day you speak to a bunch of deranged dolls.

Finally, after agreeing that was the weirdest thing either of us had ever experienced, we crept quietly back to our bedroom and looked out the window.

We arrived just in time to see Miss Ashton holding open a passage in the cedar hedge as the other dolls passed through.

"What are they going to do?" Lucy asked.

"You were there. She said she wants to impress some powerful ghost, something called the Wisp, so she can return to her human form," I said, trying to remember everything Miss Ashton had said. It wasn't easy, seeing as it was off-the-wall nuts. "And the six dolls need to return to the field where the school once stood so that Wisp thing can free them from the dolls."

"That's not what I meant," Lucy said with a shake of her head. "What do you think they're going to do once they've done all that?"

"I don't want to think about it," I admitted. "I think we should listen to Miss Ashton and stay away from them. Let them do whatever it is they want."

"But she said Grandma started the fire. What if they take their anger out on us once they're able?"

"Hopefully we'll be gone by then." But that hope didn't give me much confidence. There were still a few days until the funeral.

"Do you think Grandma actually started the fire?" Lucy asked. "They were probably lying, right?"

"Probably," I said, no longer sure about anything.

Lucy sighed. "Why don't we do what Miss Ashton said and check for ourselves?" She pointed at the journal.

Did I actually want to know? What if I didn't like the truth? I nodded in agreement anyway. My stomach felt heavy and tight, like I'd eaten a bowl of lead for supper. My fingers didn't want to cooperate, but my brain eventually got them to open the notebook and flip through the pages until I landed on an entry that caught my attention.

"Oh, no," I said.

CHAPTER 16

"WHAT IS IT?" LUCY ASKED. She peered over my shoulder at the journal.

I didn't answer. I didn't know how. After reading the first few sentences, the words couldn't find their way from my brain to my mouth, or maybe my brain couldn't form the words to begin with.

Lucy and I read in silence together.

Dear Diary,

I have tried to write this many times but it is so hard. I dont want to say what I did or even think it. I did something really, really, REALLY bad.

I burned down my school.

You know I wanted to be frends with Hattie, Mary, Dorothy, Virginia, Lois, and Ruby even if they were sometimes mean to me. And eventho I tattled on them about the cookies (Miss Ashton didnt beleve me when I told her what the girls had done, but Miss Ashton is not very nice) I stil wanted to be frends.

So three nights ago I took Daddy's keys and snuck into the school when everyone was asleep. I lit a candel so I would not need to turn on lites and wake someone. Hattie and the other girls were fast asleep in the dorm and did not hear me at all. I just wanted to take something from them so when they were looking for it I could give it back and tell them I found there things in the bathroom or something and maybe they would thank me and be happy.

I did not know what I would take but when I saw there dolls I knew that was what I would take. I grabbed each doll off the girls beds and ran to the music room.

I should have left and gone home but something about the dolls made me want to play with them right away. I pretended that Hatties doll was actualy Hattie, and that the other dolls were actualy the other girls too and we were all frends.

Reading that broke my heart into tiny pieces, and I had to take a deep breath before going any further.

They were a weerd mix of dolls but I didnt

care. It was so nice and made me so happy but only for a short time, becuz I heard a loud crash and I grabbed the dolls and ran out of the room. I was scared that Miss Ashton had found me.

I hid the dolls in the hedge between my house and the school and that is when I first smelled the smoke.

All of the sky was brite and orange but it wasn't the sunrise. The school was on fire. Daddy rushed out of our house and yelled at me to get home to safety. And that is when I rememberd the candel. I must have nocked it over when I ran out of the music room.

The fire was all my fault.

Grandma did it. She started the fire.

Accidents happen. But never in a million years would I have guessed that Grandma could have done something like that—not so much the fire, but hiding the fact that she had been responsible. Innocent people had died because of her, and she'd never told anyone the truth.

I hated to admit it, but I understood why Miss Ashton and the girls were upset with her still.

The room suddenly felt a little colder than usual, causing me to shiver and rub my arms. The house spun around me, and I needed to sit down to steady myself.

"I can't believe it," Lucy said.

"Me neither," I whispered. I felt like the world had flipped upside down. "C'mon, let's go back to bed." I couldn't think of anything else to do.

CHAPTER 17

I HAVE NO IDEA HOW she did it, but Lucy fell asleep nearly as soon as her head hit the pillow.

My mind was racing far too quickly for me to close my eyes to sleep. I couldn't turn off my thoughts. I pictured Grandma playing with the other girls' dolls all alone. I saw her knock her candle over and start the fire. I stood next to her as she watched the flames consume the school and everyone who hadn't managed to escape. I heard her dad yell at her to get home to safety. I felt the guilt that must have weighed so heavily on her for the rest of her years, and I was amazed she was able to keep such a monumentally large secret to herself.

I also replayed the events of my own bizarre night over and over in my head. I saw Sadie Sees come to life. I heard the pitter-patter of tiny feet running across the attic. And I felt the fear of... well, of everything I'd experienced earlier. It had been the scariest night of my life. I finally drifted off to sleep sometime not too long before sunrise, but I was far too disturbed and bothered to get any decent, unbroken rest. My mind jolted me out of sleep every fifteen minutes or so.

At some point my parents poked their heads into the bedroom. I pretended to be sound asleep because I was so groggy I didn't think I'd be able to form words. They must have decided not to wake us, because the next thing I heard was the sound of the car pulling out of the driveway.

Then my mind turned back to Grandma's

trunk. Was it possible Grandma knew the true nature of what it held? Is that why she got so angry with me all those years ago? I decided to see if Grandma had written about it. Reading one of her journals had provided some answers once already, even if I wasn't happy with what I'd discovered, so there was a chance it might help again.

Lucy still hadn't woken up, so I slipped soundlessly out of bed and made my way back to the attic.

As soon as I entered the room, a feeling of unease crawled over my skin like swarming ants. I grabbed the flashlight and turned it on, then crossed to the bookcase, trying to avoid looking at the open trunk in the corner. I scanned the dates on the journal spines. I pulled out the journal from the year I'd first opened the trunk. Grandma no longer began each entry with "Dear Diary," as she had when she was a child, but I did find what I was looking for.

Had a close call yesterday. Zelda opened the trunk. I yelled at her—mostly out of fear but a little out of anger, too. Anger not directed at my granddaughter, of course, but at what she had almost unwittingly released.

I heard them. Later that night, even though the trunk was sealed. Their voices were tiny and muffled, so I had to hold my breath and lean in close, but I heard them. I wish I hadn't. Their voices brought back memories I've worked too hard to repress.

And what they said was...well, it was ghastly. They spoke about waking up.

They spoke about something called the Wisp. They spoke about Zelda, and how she looked so much like I did at that age. They spoke about killing her as soon as they could. But then Mary told the others that killing someone might get the

Wisp's attention, but doing something a little more unusual might work even better—appeal to the Wisp's sense of justice. "An eye for an eye," Mary said. They want to turn Zelda into a doll, sew up her mouth and her nose and her eyes and let her slowly drift away into a doll-like slumber.

I still don't know why the dolls can't get out of the trunk on their own. I suspect it has something to do with the chalcedony stones in the lid. Whatever it is, I'm thankful for it.

Zelda was upset when I yelled at her. And no wonder. I felt terrible. I went out and bought her a bright, shiny new doll, and I gave it to her this morning. It seemed to help improve her mood. It made me feel a little better, but only a little.

Thank goodness those dolls are trapped in that trunk. I can't bear to think what they might do if they ever escaped.

They wanted to turn me into a doll.

It all clicked.

After Lucy had opened the trunk, when Miss Ashton had said to wait until there was only one, she'd been referring to me and my sister. And when Hattie had wanted to do it now, she'd wanted to kill one of us—maybe both of us. But Miss Ashton stopped her.

Because she wanted to wait until one of us was alone. And she didn't want to kill us—at least, not quickly. She wanted to use needle and thread to turn me into some sort of sick human doll.

I was suddenly overcome by the uncontrollable desire to rejoin my sister immediately and to not let her out of my sight for the rest of our time in Summerside. I raced down the stairs two or three at a time and barged into our room.

Lucy was gone.

CHAPTER 18

"LUCY!" I YELLED AT THE top of my lungs. "Lucy!"

I searched the other bedroom and the bathroom. She wasn't there. I tore down the stairs to the main floor shouting her name. No response. Then I found the kitchen door open, and I knew my fears were correct. Miss Ashton and the girls had waited until the perfect time to take my sister.

The sun beat down as I sprinted across the empty backyard. I lunged through the hedge without slowing down, using my shoulder as a battering ram and crashing through to the other side.

Despite my frantic sense of urgency, what I found on the other side made me stop dead.

It was the school—Summerside School, standing where it once had, before my grandmother had accidentally burned it down.

The school looked exactly as it had in the newspaper picture. Tall, dark, made of stone and as intimidating as any building I'd ever seen.

I felt like I was dreaming. I couldn't believe my eyes.

Maybe, I realized, the dream I'd had the night I'd first opened the trunk back when I was nine years old hadn't been a dream after all.

As much as I wanted to knock down the doors and run into the school, I approached the building slowly. I didn't want Miss Ashton and the girls to know I was coming. If Lucy was in there, I didn't want to put her in danger.

The bell tower loomed above me and the composition of the windows on either side of the front door seemed to form a large face that stared out at the world, daring me to enter.

I noticed something odd as I walked: an optical illusion or a trick of the light. The building appeared to take on a translucent glow.

I stopped. The building looked solid. I took a few steps. Its surface became see-through again.

It's a ghost school, I thought. It made no sense, but then again nothing made sense anymore. Spirits were real. Dolls walked and talked. Burned-down schools rose from the ashes. The world as I knew it had flipped. I felt like I was suddenly inhabiting a parallel dimension.

Would I be able to enter the school? Or would I fall through the floor as soon as I set foot on it? I had no idea, but there was only one way to find out. I needed to find my sister. There was no time to waste. My parents weren't home, and I doubted the police would believe me if I told them the ghosts of a headmistress and six girls had possessed seven dolls and were hiding out in their school, which had burned down more than sixty years ago.

I was on my own. And I'd already decided I couldn't just hide and hope for the best. So that left one option. I had to go in and see whether or not I fell through the floor. And then, regardless, I had to find Lucy.

The temperature dropped a few degrees as I walked up the steps to the front door, and the hair on my arms and the back of my neck stood on end. The air felt heavy, and I heard a low hum. It was as if the school was alive with electricity. I felt a little nauseous. I took a deep breath, but that only made things worse; there was a hint of something gaseous in the air, like rotten eggs mixed in with the smell of charcoal, and inhaling that pungent mix was awful. I tried to take quicker, shallower breaths but it didn't help much.

I gripped and turned the door handle—it was

ice cold—and pushed the door. It swung open easily.

I had the feeling that the school was an active participant in this mess, leading me on. It felt like a trap. Despite this concerning thought, I stepped inside.

My foot touched the floor. I didn't fall through.

So far, so good.

Both the gassy smell and the burning smell faded away and were replaced by a musty smell, like the place needed to be aired out. That struck me as weird, because only a short while ago this whole lot was an open, airy field.

The school's interior was nothing like any school I'd ever seen. The foyer was very small. Across from the entrance was a staircase, and a hallway ran on either side of it. To the left was the library and to the right was a bathroom and a lounge. Everything was made of dark wood, the furniture was all antique, and old-fashioned decorations covered every surface. Large portraits in ornate gold frames filled the walls. Each painting was of a stern-looking woman staring out at me. The nameplate on the portrait closest to the staircase identified the subject as Miss Ashton. Compared to the others, she actually didn't look as mean and intimidating.

As I examined the painting, a chilling sound from above caught my attention—half shuffle, half scrape, like a body being dragged across the floor. And then I heard Miss Ashton's singsong voice flutter down to me.

"Come out, come out, wherever you are!"

CHAPTER 19

ALTHOUGH I'D IMPRESSED MYSELF WITH my bravery up to that point, I nearly lost my nerve and ran out of the school with my tail tucked between my legs. But then I remembered why I'd come. My sister needed me.

As long as it's not her body being dragged across the floor upstairs, I thought morbidly. *As long as I'm not too late.*

I shook my head—I couldn't think like that. I reached for an old candlestick off a side table and was a bit surprised that my hand didn't pass straight through it. I shook the candle free, and it clattered to the floor.

I felt better holding it, even if it wasn't much of a weapon. There was a second candlestick that matched the first on the side table, so I picked it up, too, and turned it upside down, freeing the candle. Two was better than one, I figured. It couldn't hurt, and Lucy would need something to defend herself if—*when*—I found her.

I looked up the stairs. The staircase wound up to the third floor.

The body-dragging sound picked up again, followed by Miss Ashton's melodic voice.

"I've got something for you," she sang.

It felt like a trap. But even if it was, that didn't matter. I had to stop Miss Ashton. And although I didn't want to destroy the doll Grandma had given me, I had a feeling that was exactly what I'd need to do. After all, Sadie Sees wasn't the only thing of hers I had. I had my memories of her, and no one—not Miss Ashton or the other dolls or anyone else—could ever take those from me. Grandma loved me, and I didn't need Sadie Sees to remind me of that.

Without wasting another moment, I climbed up the stairs with one of the candlesticks raised and ready to strike. The dragging sound was louder when I reached the second floor, but it was still coming from above. I carried on to the third floor.

A long hall stretched out to the left and the right, interrupted by a dozen doors that led, I guessed, to classrooms. But which room was Miss Ashton hidden in? More important, where was Lucy?

"I have a feeling you're going to love this," came Miss Ashton's voice from behind a door at the end of the hall.

I ran to the door and threw it open.

Lit candles ringed the room, the flickering flames reflecting brightly on brass musical instruments and casting dancing shadows on the walls. The flames, though, were cool blue—not yellow—making the room appear to be lit by moonlight instead of candlelight. Sadie Sees, still possessed by Miss Ashton, stood in the center of the room, smiling and laughing like a maniac. She waved her tiny plastic arms in the air above her head, and the instruments—as if they too were possessed—began to play a soft, haunting melody all on their own.

The six girls—still inside their old, creepy dolls—stood to the side of the room. They whipped their heads in my direction. None of them looked happy to see me.

I didn't care. Let them look at me. Let them glare. It didn't matter.

The only thing I cared about was that Lucy was there, too. She was tied to a chair in the center of the room. She didn't appear harmed in any way. As she caught sight of me her eyes brightened hopefully, but I could tell she was holding herself back from calling out.

Then I noticed that Hattie, the perfect-looking doll, held a threaded sewing needle.

Something dawned on me. Miss Ashton hadn't been enticing me up to the third floor in an attempt to trap me. She'd been calling that eternal spirit she'd mentioned, the one who could give them all their bodies back. The Wisp. The music Miss Ashton had summoned was the séance she had mentioned. And they were about to turn my sister into a doll.

There was no time to lose. I threw one of the candlesticks at Miss Ashton. She ducked beneath it, and it clanged loudly on the floor behind her. I had missed, but throwing the candlestick hadn't been a complete waste. The instruments around her fell to the floor thanks to the distraction.

She stood up straight and spun around. The blue fire flickered in her wide eyes. She looked ready to murder me.

And as it turned out, she was.

She looked at the other six dolls, then back to me.

"Kill her," she said.

CHAPTER 20

THE SIGHT OF SIX POSSESSED dolls racing toward me was the stuff of nightmares, so disturbing that I temporarily forgot to breathe.

Hattie tossed her needle and thread aside and led the charge, her curly red hair bobbing with every stride and her blue eyes boring into me. Mary, the baby doll, was to Hattie's left, crawling on her hands and knees with unnatural speed. Dorothy was to Hattie's right, glaring at me through her old wire-framed glasses. The other three dolls ran together in a row behind Hattie. Virginia's internal organs jostled in her belly, threatening to spill out onto the floor. Unlike the others', Lois's oversized eyes didn't seem capable of looking angry, which was somehow worse. And Ruby's wooden joints click-clacked as she ran, sounding like a mix of exploding firecrackers and brittle bones being snapped in half.

I wished I had something heavier to protect myself with, like a bat or a crowbar, but I swung the second candlestick at Hattie like a tennis racket. It connected and sent her flying through the air. She hit the far wall and broke apart into six large pieces—two arms, two legs, one torso and one decapitated head—that rained down on the floor.

The other dolls stopped dead in their tracks and looked concerned that Hattie had been so easily defeated.

I laughed in victory. "That's right! Come near

me and I'll smash you to bits and pieces." But then my smile fell.

One of Hattie's arms began to shake, and then the fingers spread apart and dug into the floor. The arm pulled itself toward the other pieces as they also sprung back to life. Her legs stood up and hopped. Her torso rolled end over end. Her eyes opened, her mouth smiled, and her head waited patiently where it lay.

Her arms snapped into place at each shoulder. Her legs slid into position beneath her waist. Then her headless body lurched over to her head, picked it up, and forced it into her empty neck hole.

I had only managed to slow Hattie down.

The other five girls swiveled their heads to face me. But they were still a little wary of the candlestick. I could see it in their eyes. I raised it as if I was about to strike, and all of them flinched.

It was now or never. I charged the girls, and they ran in opposite directions, so I changed course and bolted toward Miss Ashton. I swung the candlestick at her, and she ducked underneath it and joined the six girls on the other side of the room.

Luckily, they hadn't tied Lucy to the chair too securely, and I was able to untie the rope quickly.

"Ready to run?" I asked her. She nodded.

We bolted for the door and slammed it shut behind us. I heard one or two of the dolls smash into it on the other side and fall to pieces—pieces I knew would simply reform and continue to chase us. How could we stop them? Like, permanently?

As much as I was trying to maintain a positive attitude, the situation was looking hopeless.

"Are you okay?" I asked Lucy.

"I've felt better."

"We have to get out of here." I pointed at the stairs halfway down the hall.

She nodded in understanding.

We raced down the hall. I heard the music

room door swing open, and the doll horde pour out into the hall behind us.

In our panic we veered too close to each other, and we bumped shoulders, causing me to drop the candlestick. It didn't matter. The stairs were only a few feet away.

I kept running. Lucy didn't.

She stopped to pick up the candlestick.

"Lucy, no!" I shouted.

The dolls closed in on her. "Leave it!" I pleaded desperately.

She didn't appear to hear me. She was rooted to the ground, her hand suspended in midair above the candlestick, staring in fear at the dolls.

Another three or four seconds, and the dolls would be on top of her.

I ran in front of her—getting between her and the immediate threat—and scooped the candlestick off the floor, then swung it to the left. The first three dolls flew off their feet and hit the wall. I swung the candlestick to the right and the next two dolls were propelled into the other wall. The sixth doll—the one with the big eyes and the cracked face—ran straight for me, so I swung the candlestick straight down on her head. She crumpled at my feet.

Miss Ashton was close behind the others. I swung the candlestick at her, but too late. She ducked and slid between my legs. She got back to her feet and jumped at Lucy. She hit my sister in the center of the chest. Lucy was rocked backward toward the stairs. Her arms spun in circles around her head as she tried to regain her balance. She took two, three, four awkward steps back. Miss Ashton fell to the ground and watched Lucy with a wicked gleam in her eyes. For an all-too-brief moment, it looked like Lucy was going to be okay.

But then her heel rolled over the edge of the top step.

And it was all over. Momentum and gravity took over.

CHAPTER 21

LUCY RAISED HER ARMS TO protect her head and tumbled down the stairs. Although it was a short distance to the landing, only six or seven steps, the sound of her crashing to a stop was painfully loud. She didn't move.

"No," someone said. Me, I realized. "No!" I shouted as I returned to my senses.

I looked from my sister's still body to Sadie Sees, standing a short distance beside me, looking down the stairs with glee. She had long ago stopped being my doll. She no longer made me think of Grandma. All I saw when I looked at her was the horrible creature that had hurt my sister. All I saw was Miss Ashton, and she needed to pay. But first, I needed to make sure Lucy was okay.

I hit Miss Ashton as hard as I could. She rocketed down the hall and landed amid the other dolls, which were getting back to their feet.

I raced down the stairs and crouched beside my sister.

"Lucy?" I said loudly beside her ear.

She didn't respond, not at first. Her eyes were closed. Her face looked pained. But then her eyelids fluttered open, and she looked at me in confusion. "What happened?"

I laughed in relief and tears sprang from my eyes. "You fell down the stairs," I said, "but you're going to be okay."

I looked back up at the third floor. The dolls and Miss Ashton stepped to the edge and stared down.

"I'm going to pick you up," I told Lucy.

I placed the candlestick on her chest, slid my arms under her body as gently as possible and scooped her up. It was a bit of a struggle—she was small for her age but she wasn't exactly light. She held on to my neck, and I found the strength to get to my feet. The fear and adrenaline coursing through my veins helped.

The dolls flowed down the stairs.

I didn't know where to go, but I started to run anyway—down the stairs to the first floor. When I saw the front door I considered rushing through it and back to Grandma's house, but I knew I had to put a stop to the dolls once and for all if I wanted to save my sister and myself. Otherwise they'd never stop coming for us.

The only thing I could think to do was find a safe place to hide while I worked things out.

The bathroom. It was worth a shot.

I ran down the front hall with Lucy in my arms, my shoulders aching and my back screaming, and pushed the bathroom door open with my hip. Once inside I laid Lucy on the floor, grabbed the candlestick, and studied the door.

It had a lock!

I turned it quickly just as I heard the dolls reach the other side. The door rattled in its frame as they pulled on it and banged against it, but it held.

I scanned the room for anything that might be useful. Nothing caught my eye. Just a row of sinks, and a small window above them.

"You can't wait in there forever," I heard Miss Ashton say from the other side. "But we can wait out here as long as necessary. We've already waited more than sixty years for this moment."

The feeling of relief that had washed over me when I'd found Lucy was replaced with a feeling of despair. We could try to squeeze through the window, but Miss Ashton and the others would probably hear us. They'd continue pursuing us forever and ever and ever until...until we were dead, and they'd summoned the Wisp. That was the only way this could end.

Knock, knock, knock.

"Little pig, little pig, let me in," Miss Ashton said, and the girls laughed.

CHAPTER 22

WE WERE TRAPPED, AND EVERYTHING had begun to feel hopeless, but at least I'd managed to get us to safety temporarily. And my sister was lucky—her fall could have been much, much worse.

"Are you okay?" I asked.

She nodded weakly. "I've got a killer headache, but I'm okay." She propped herself up on one elbow and winced in pain.

"Are you hurt anywhere?" I asked.

"I'm hurt everywhere," she said.

It was good to see she was able to joke. "I think you were unconscious for a bit."

She placed her fingertips gently on her forehead. "Yeah, I was, and I had an awful dream while I was passed out."

"What was it about?"

"I was here in the school a long time ago. Grandma was in the music room playing with the dolls she'd borrowed."

"*Stolen*," one of the girls—Mary, the baby doll, I thought—said from the other side of the door.

Lucy continued. "She heard a noise and ran away, just like she said in her journal. The candle tipped over. The flames spread quickly. It was awful."

I nodded in agreement, feeling some of the guilt—probably a tiny fraction of what Grandma had felt all her life—for what had happened here back in 1952. I looked at the candlestick and realized I was squeezing it so tight that my knuckles had turned red and white. Maybe it was the same one Grandma had used to light her way that night.

Hattie's laughter came through the door.

"You think the school burning is funny?" I said in disgust. "People died."

"I was one of those people," Hattie said. "But that's not why I'm laughing. I'm laughing at Edith thinking all these years the fire was her fault."

"What do you mean?" Lucy asked. "She didn't do it."

"Who did?" I asked, even though I had a pretty good guess.

"I did."

I was about to ask if she was serious, but Miss Ashton beat me to it.

"*You* set the fire?" she asked.

"Not on purpose," Hattie said, somehow managing to sound offended. "I saw Edith steal our dolls, so I followed her to the music room and hid and watched. She looked so pathetic playing with our dolls and pretending they were us that I almost felt bad for her. When I knocked over a cymbal, she ran out of the room with the dolls in her arms. I chased after her, but I ran too close to the candle she'd left behind. It tipped over and rolled under one of the drapes. It caught fire quickly. I tried putting it out but realized I wouldn't be able to on my own, so I ran for the door but..." She sighed irritably. "I tripped, fell, and everything went black. The next thing I knew I was floating through the smoky sky above the school when I spotted the other girls, floating through the air with me. And then I saw Edith and her *caretaker* father, doing nothing but watch the school burn."

The way Hattie said "caretaker" made it sound like a swear word, something vile in her mouth that needed to be spat out.

"I also spotted our dolls—she'd hid them in the hedge," Hattie continued. "And so, instead of passing on, I had the idea to slip into my doll. And it worked. The other girls followed my lead. But before we could do anything—before we had the strength to act—Edith hid us in her trunk, and those red stones in the lid kept us trapped in there ever since."

It wasn't Grandma's fault. I felt like a giant weight had been lifted off my shoulders. I wished there was some way I could tell her. I almost felt happy enough to cry. It gave me the strength I needed to figure out a way to beat the dolls.

"Why didn't you say anything before?" Miss Ashton asked. Her tone was icy cold. Without seeing her I couldn't tell if she was angry or simply dumbfounded.

"Edith shouldn't have been in class with us," Hattie said. "The only reason she'd been granted admission was because her father worked for the school. And to think she wanted to be our friend." She laughed bitterly.

None of the other girls joined in her laughter,

which gave me a small shred of satisfaction. And then I had an idea.

I motioned soundlessly for Lucy to follow me into one of the bathroom stalls. We crammed inside the small space and I closed the door, hoping that would create a bit of a sound barrier. I didn't want the dolls to hear us.

"I think I know how to beat them," I whispered, "but for my plan to work, you have to stay in here." Lucy opened her mouth to protest, but I cut her off. "You have to stay in here, Lucy. It's the only way, and I don't have time to explain. I'm going to run out, and you need to lock the door behind me. No matter what you hear or what happens next, don't follow me. Wait five minutes, then climb out the bathroom window. Go back to our bedroom in Grandma's house and watch out the window. And this is the most important part: if you see any of the dolls, or any ghosts enter the backyard, run up to the attic and hide in the trunk. They won't be able to get to you in there.

Do you understand?" Lucy's eyes were red and her bottom lip quivered, but she nodded.

"Tell me you'll get out, no matter what you see or hear."

"I will," Lucy said. She squinted and added, "You too, right?"

I nodded and looked away. "Of course."

"Okay," she said, looking a little relieved.

"Hey, come here." I pulled her close and hugged her tight. "We're going to be okay."

"Promise?"

It broke my heart to lie to my sister, but I forced a smile and said, "Promise."

CHAPTER 23

WE PULLED APART AND GAVE each other one final look. I could only hope she'd do exactly as I'd said. There was so much that could go wrong. I felt like I was standing on top of a house of highly flammable cards, soaked in gasoline, about to strike a match.

"All right," I said. "It's time. Ready?"

"Ready."

We left the stall. I picked up the candlestick and reached for the dead bolt on the bathroom door. Outside I could hear the dolls scratching at the door, trying to find a way in.

I looked at Lucy and raised one finger off the candlestick.

One.

I raised a second.

Two.

And then, after I raised a third—*three!*—I nodded, tightened my grip on the candlestick, unlocked the dead bolt, threw open the door, and charged out into the hall. The door bashed one or two dolls to the side. I used the candlestick to hit a few more. I think I kicked one as I started to run, but it was hard to be sure. Everything was a blur. But I distinctly heard the click of the lock on the door behind me.

"You don't honestly think you can escape us, do you?" Miss Ashton asked incredulously.

"I'm pretty sure I'm faster than a pathetic old lady that has to live inside a kid's toy," I said, hoping my words would antagonize her.

Luckily for me, they did. Big-time.

She lunged for me, enraged. I swerved around her outstretched arms and bolted up the stairs, all the way to the third floor without stopping to catch my breath or look behind me. I knew Miss Ashton was following me, and I knew the others were following close behind her. I ran down the hall, barged into the music room, and dragged a desk to the side of the door. Although a big part of me wanted to use the desk to block the door and prevent the dolls from entering the room, I left it where it was. They would expect me to barricade them out, and to ensure I outwitted the dolls, I knew I needed to do something they'd never see coming in a million years. Something unthinkable.

The door opened, and the dolls poured in. I pushed myself up against the wall beside the desk, out of their sight.

Miss Ashton entered first, followed by Mary, Dorothy, Virginia, Lois, Ruby...

I held my breath. Had Hattie stayed downstairs to try to get into the bathroom, as I'd feared might happen? But then, a moment later, Hattie finally ran into the music room and joined the others.

I slammed the door shut and pushed the desk in front of it.

"What are you doing?" Miss Ashton shrieked.

I ignored her and swapped my candlestick for one of the lit candles from the séance Miss Ashton had begun earlier. Then I grabbed one of the drapes from the closest window.

Miss Ashton raised her hands and took a step toward me. Understanding dawned on her face.

"You don't want to do that," she said. "You're trapped in here with us. Set fire to the room and you'll die, too."

I hesitated for a moment. Could I actually follow through with what I had planned?

As if she picked up on my last-minute hesitation, Hattie smiled and taunted me. "Go ahead, set us all on fire. See how you like to burn. See how you like to be torn apart from your family and stuck between worlds for years."

The way she spoke angered me—she'd started the original fire, but she managed to make it sound like she was the victim. Not to mention the fact that a moment ago she'd been ready to sew Lucy up like a doll. It was for Lucy that I had to see my plan through to the bitter end.

I lit the bottom of the drape on fire then ripped it free from the rod above the window. I balled the flaming material up and threw it at the dolls. The look on Hattie's face, as well as the others', was priceless. None of them thought I'd actually set fire to the room while I was trapped in it with them, but they were wrong.

While they were scrambling, I ran around the room knocking the other candles over and setting fire to anything I could find.

The fire spread quickly, far more quickly than I would've thought possible. The dolls tried to avoid the flames but they couldn't forever. Soon they were all burning blue, and they shrieked and howled and wailed as they ran in circles, spreading the fire farther around the room. I didn't know whether Miss Ashton and the girls felt the pain of burning alive, or if they were remembering the first time they'd been burned, or if they were simply terrified of fading away permanently. Whatever the case, one by one they began to slow down and fall as their bodies were consumed by the fire. Hattie tried to pull the desk away from the door in a last-ditch effort to save herself, but Miss Ashton pulled her back.

"What are you doing?" I asked the headmistress.

"Helping you," Miss Ashton said as her face melted. "Stopping her from escaping."

"Why?" I said.

"I thought your grandmother burned down my school, but it was her." She pointed at Hattie.

"All these years my anger has been focused on the wrong person."

Plastic melted and dripped off her body in thick rivulets, and she fell to the ground and stared at me. Her hair and clothes had burned away first, and I could see the mechanics that made her eyes and mouth move inside her head. It was the stuff of nightmares.

"I can see through aaannnyyythiiinggg..." she said in Sadie's prerecorded voice, her speech box malfunctioning and dying.

And then she was silent.

The flames licked closer all around me. My cheeks were flushed and sweat poured down my body.

All of the old dolls had stopped moving and were little more than piles of melted plastic and burned wood. All except Hattie. She was somehow still hanging on, but just barely.

My lungs burned, and I coughed violently. The smell of burning plastic was horrible. I crouched low to the ground to try to avoid breathing it in.

"I can see," Hattie said, echoing one of Sadie Sees's sayings. "I can see. I can see. I can see... that this will all be for naught. I'm going to—"

She didn't finish her final threat. Her jaw fell off and her body crumpled in on itself. Within a few more seconds she was reduced to nothing more than a flaming puddle of sludge.

"Good riddance," I choked out.

My head swam and I felt like I was about to throw up, but at least my plan had worked. I closed my eyes and hoped that Lucy had made it out to safety.

She made it, I told myself.

Amid the crackle of the fire I heard glass shatter. I raised my head and opened my eyes. A rock rattled across the floor. It had come from the window. I peered through the smoke and saw that the window was broken.

"Zelda!" I heard someone shout. Lucy. Outside. "Zelda!"

I stumbled a little but got to my feet. I was shaky but managed to make my way through the fire to the broken window. The air smelled fresh and sweet. I looked outside.

Standing on the grass below were Lucy, Mom, and Dad. Lucy must've gotten them instead of going straight to the bedroom. The three of them looked absolutely panic-stricken. It made me realize how foolish I'd been. I hadn't considered the impact my actions would have on my family.

"Mom! Dad! Help me!" I shouted.

"Hang on, Zelda!" Mom said. She unfolded something and handed the edges to Dad and Lucy. A large white blanket off Grandma's bed. They spread out, pulled the blanket taut, and created a safety net to catch me in.

"Jump!" Mom yelled.

I didn't hesitate. I jumped.

CHAPTER 24

I HADN'T CONSIDERED MYSELF TO be afraid of heights before, but three days after I had jumped from the burning school I still felt tense when I thought about the second or two I spent in free fall.

"Zelda? You okay?"

It was Lucy, snapping me out of my daydream. More like daymare.

"What?" I said, confused for a moment as the memory of jumping out the third-floor window switched to my immediate surroundings. We were sitting in Grandma's family room. My parents, uncles, aunts, and cousins were in small groups throughout the house having quiet conversations. I rubbed my eyes and straightened my black dress. "Yes, I'm fine. Just zoned out a little."

"Still thinking about it?" Lucy asked.

"Every now and again," I said, an understatement. How could I think of anything else? I imagined I'd be thinking about it for the rest of my life.

Lucy nodded in sympathy. She'd probably remember that day for the rest of her life, too, and she'd probably be the only person who would ever fully understand what I—what we—went through. We told Mom and Dad, and they'd believed every word—they'd seen the school, after all, as well as the blue flames that burned it to the ground but left no trace of cinders or ash once the building was gone. But they hadn't been there with us. They hadn't spoken with Miss Ashton, and they hadn't been attacked by the dolls. They hadn't lost a few hours of their lives—I estimated we were in the school for a little less than an hour, but when we finally returned to Grandma's house the sun was already beginning to set. I should've told them what was happening from the start even if they wouldn't have believed a word. Live and learn, I guess. At least I *had* lived.

The thought drew my attention back to the casket at the far side of the living room. Grandma had stated in her will that she wanted her funeral to be in her own house. No one had been surprised by that—Grandma loved any opportunity to gather family and friends in her home.

The casket was open. I knew Grandma was inside, but I hadn't approached it yet. Not because I was afraid of seeing her that way, but because I assumed Lucy probably was.

I stood up slowly. "Well, what do you say? Think you're ready to go say goodbye to Grandma now?"

She frowned as she stood beside me. "Me? I've

been wanting to go up since the start. I thought you needed time to prepare yourself."

I laughed and placed a hand on Lucy's back. "C'mon, let's go."

Dad saw us approach the casket and elbowed Mom. They looked at us with sad smiles. I smiled back.

I rested my hands on the edge of the casket and looked at Grandma. She was wearing one of her favorite dresses, a white one covered in sunflowers. She wore more makeup than usual—I didn't think she'd like that—but she looked good. Her eyes were closed, and her hands were crossed over her belly.

Tears sprang to my eyes, surprising me, as I felt a flush creep up my neck. Once more I thought of square sandwiches and fishing bait and tomatoes and bedtime stories.

"I just want you to know the fire wasn't your fault, Grandma," I said. "And sorry I read your journal."

Lucy laughed in relief and started to cry at the same time. I put an arm around her and she rested her head on my shoulder.

"I love you, and I'll miss you," she told Grandma. I thought back to something that had crossed my mind just before I went into the ghost school. "We have our memories, and no one can take those away. As long as we remember Grandma, she'll always be with us."

Lucy wiped away her tears and nodded.

We were silent for a moment, sharing time with Grandma and each other.

I thought of a few texts Camryn had sent me earlier in the morning that I hadn't answered yet.

Sorry about ur grandma

Sorry I was a jerk about ur doll nbd 2 me if u keep her lol

Maybe I'd tell Camryn one day the real story of what happened to Sadie Sees, but for now it was nice that she'd reached out to make amends.

Thinking of Sadie made me think again of all

the dolls melting in the music room and brought a smile to my lips.

But then I saw a twitch of movement out of the corner of my eye that wiped the smile clean off my face.

The movement had come from inside the casket.

It was probably nothing, I thought. *It was definitely nothing.*

"C'mon," I said to Lucy, trying to force the smile back as I guided her away from Grandma's casket. "Let's go sit down and try to never think of dolls again."

Joel A. Sutherland is the author of *Be a Writing Superstar*, numerous volumes of the Haunted Canada series (which received the Silver Birch Award and the Hackmatack Award), *Summer's End* (finalist for the Red Maple Award) and *Frozen Blood*, a horror novel that was nominated for the Bram Stoker Award. His short fiction has appeared in many anthologies and magazines, including *Blood Lite II & III* and *Cemetery Dance* magazine, alongside the likes of Stephen

King and Neil Gaiman. He has been a juror for the John Spray Mystery Award and the Monica Hughes Award for Science Fiction and Fantasy.

He is a children's and youth services librarian and appeared as "The Barbarian Librarian" on the Canadian edition of the hit television show *Wipeout*, making it all the way to the third round and proving that librarians can be just as tough and wild as anyone else.

Joel lives with his family in southeastern Ontario, where he is always on the lookout for ghosts.

Read all the books in the Haunted series!

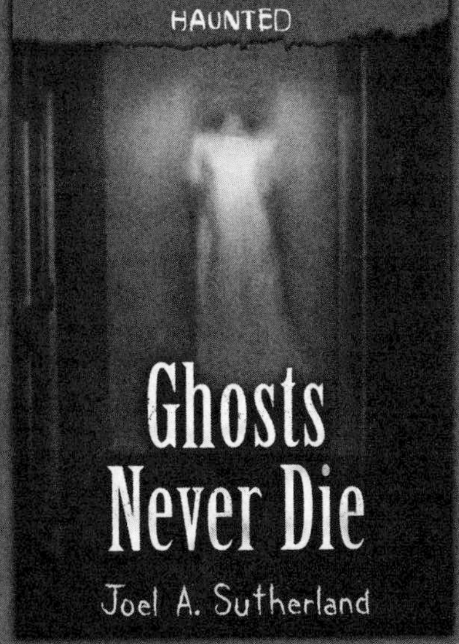

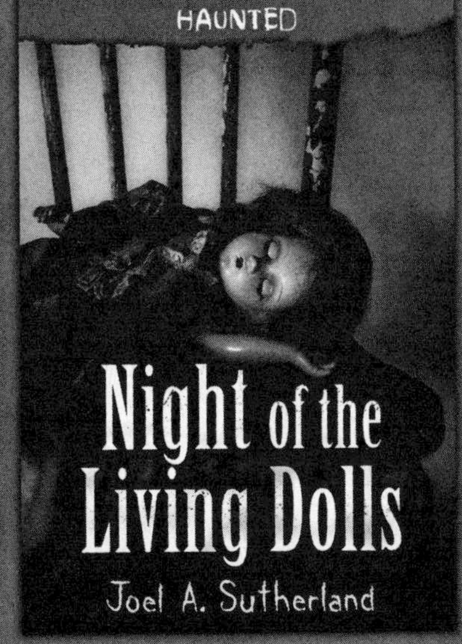